"What if I won't stay?" Claire asked

Terrill frowned. "Then I'll lock you in this room until you agree. I may ravish you a few times for good measure. It's time you learned to act like a woman."

He suddenly bent his head and kissed her lips firmly. "There. Didn't hurt much, did it?"

Claire stifled a giggle at the idea that she minded at all, though she looked at him reprovingly.

"Does your unusual lack of a reply mean you'll stay?"

"Oh, all right, I'll stay," Claire said, making her voice sound grudging, knowing he'd have to carry her kicking and screaming to the airport if he wanted her to go.

"Does your reluctant agreement indicate a desire to be helpful, or a strong desire not to be ravished anytime soon?" he asked. Claire couldn't possibly answer that one.

Katherine Arthur is full of life. She describes herself as a writer, research associate (she works with her husband, a research professor in experimental psychology), farmer, housewife, proud mother of five and a grandmother to boot. The family is definitely full of overachievers. But what she finds most interesting is the diversity of occupations the children have chosen—sports medicine, computers, finance and neuroscience (pioneering brain tissue transplants), to name a few. Why, the possibilities for story ideas are practically limitless.

Remember, in Jamaica

Katherine Arthur

Harlequin Books

TORONTO • NEW YORK • LONDON
AMSTERDAM • PARIS • SYDNEY • HAMBURG
STOCKHOLM • ATHENS • TOKYO • MILAN

Original hardcover edition published in 1988
by Mills & Boon Limited

ISBN 0-373-02971-3

Harlequin Romance first edition April 1989

CHAPTER ONE

CLAIRE FORSYTHE leaned forward, her elbows propped on her desk blotter, the square jaw and pointed chin that Terrill Hawkes frequently described as stubborn jutting dangerously.

'You want me to leave for Jamaica tomorrow?' she purred in a voice scalloped with icicles.

'I suppose it's a little late to get a flight today,' that same Terrill Hawkes replied with an exaggerated shrug. He tipped his chair precariously backwards and crossed one leg over the other, giving Claire an unconcerned smile that she categorised as his 'I'm the boss' smirk.

With her eyes narrowed and her carefully manicured fingernails drumming an angry cadence on her desk, Claire considered the impeccably groomed man seated across from her. Even his custom-tailored suit could not disguise the strong neck and big shoulders of the professional football player he had been before an injury had ended that career. She could picture him, leaping forward, grabbing an opponent, and flinging him to the ground. Crash! Wham! Thump! Bang! That was still his style. Come hell or high water, he ploughed straight ahead.

Not five minutes ago he had come striding into her office, without knocking as usual, and announced, 'Miss Forsythe, I finally found a property in the right location in Jamaica. It's run-down and needs a lot of work, but with you in charge it will become the star in the line-up of Hawkes Hotels and Resorts. Our first overseas venture. I want you to get right down there and start the wheels in motion. You can stay at my villa. I already called my housekeeper and told her to be expecting you tomorrow.'

Why did it never, ever, occur to him that she might have other plans? More to the point at the moment, had he really forgotten that he had promised her a vacation when she finished her most recent project, or was he simply ignoring the fact? She suspected it was the latter. He was planning to bury her vacation in a pile of projects, like the defensive football team burying the ball carrier in a pile of bodies. Well, this time it wasn't going to work. The only question was what strategy it would take to get the overpowering Mr Hawkes to realise that fact.

The pause lengthened while Claire continued to glower, Terrill Hawkes to smirk, and she debated whether she should quit immediately or wait until they had shouted at each other for a few minutes. Wait, she decided. She looked away and fingered an ear-ring thoughtfully.

'I can't go,' she said flatly.

'Why, Miss Forsythe,' Terrill Hawkes said, unfolding his legs and allowing his chair to return to all fours with an agonised screech of its overstrained joints, 'I didn't think the word "can't" was in your vocabulary.'

While Claire watched knowingly, the smirk was exchanged for the familiar, wide-eyed, 'I don't believe what I'm hearing' stare.

'Can't,' Claire repeated. 'As in I can't believe

you don't remember you promised me a vacation after I finished the Hawkes' Nest at Lake Tahoe.' Her voice rose several decibels. 'As in I can't go because I didn't even get home to see my family at Christmas and *they* are expecting me tomorrow.'

There was another oversized shrug. 'Surely they can do without you for a little longer. Being in Jamaica is a vacation in itself, especially in mid-winter. You'll love it there. And once you get the plans approved and the contractors hired you can take a few days off and fly home.'

'Mr Hawkes,' Claire said, gritting her teeth in the face of another smirk, 'you are not listening to me. Perhaps I should phrase it differently. I *will* not go tomorrow. I am going home for two weeks. Jamaica will have to wait.'

Terrill Hawkes looked down and flicked an invisible speck of lint from his deep blue suit.

'Miss Forsythe,' he said, without looking up, 'how long have you been working for me?'

Aha! Claire thought. Her message was getting through. Terrill Hawkes always avoided looking her in the eye when he knew he was in the wrong. Now they could get down to some serious arguing. She looked up and studied the ceiling.

'Three years, give or take a few weeks,' she replied, sighing heavily. 'I guess it only *seems* like three hundred.' She lowered her head, pounded her desk, and shouted, 'Because I *never* get any time off, Prisoners in the Gulag have more time off than I do!' Which was a bit of an exaggeration, but Terrill Hawkes was not one to respond to simple, straightforward logic.

Terrill Hawkes' blue eyes lighted with what Claire had come to call the 'orator instructing the ill-

informed masses' gleam, which meant that he was
preparing to classify all of her arguments as
meaningless against the overwhelming rightness of
his own.

'I doubt if time is of the essence when you're
bashing rocks, or whatever they do,' he growled, at
first softly and then with increasing force as he
continued, 'However, I assume, perhaps wrongly,
that by now you are aware that time is money in the
hotel business, and that every day that the Jamaica
property stands empty of customers I am losing
thousands of dollars?' The 'thousands of dollars'
came out at a low roar.

'I am,' Claire replied serenely. 'I can practically
envisage the wolf gnawing at your coat-tails.' She
smiled, as if the thought gave her great pleasure.
Was it time to remind dear Mr Hawkes that it would
take him more than two weeks to replace her? No,
not quite yet. 'Perhaps if you stick to black bread
and gruel instead of porterhouse steaks for a month
or two you can make it up,' she suggested instead. 'I
am going home tomorrow. For two weeks. Period.'

'One week!' Terrill Hawkes shouted, jumping to
his feet.

'Two!' Claire shouted back, not flinching as he
folded his arms across his chest and glared at her.
Unless she missed her guess, she was almost there.

'I don't have to put up with this,' he snarled.
'You can take your blasted two weeks and the rest of
your life for all I care. You're fired!'

'Good!' Claire reached for the tote-bag she always
kept beneath her desk, jerked open one of the
drawers, and started unloading the contents into the
bag. 'Good luck in finding my replacement. It
shouldn't take you more than a few months.' If he

could ever find one who would put up with him, it would be a miracle, she added to herself. Not that she thought she was really fired this time.

'It would be worth it, not to have to put up with a stubborn shrew like you,' Terrill Hawkes said, his voice returning to a more conversational pitch.

Claire paused in her unloading and jerked her chin up. 'Did I just hear you call me a stubborn shrew?' she enquired on an ascending scale. She jumped to her feet and leaned forward menacingly. 'Did I?' she yelled, with the screech of a cat whose tail has been trod upon.

'You did!'

'That does it!' A coffee mug joined the articles in the tote-bag with such force that it shattered loudly. 'I'll take three weeks off instead of two.'

'Take all eternity!' came the thunderous reply. Terrill Hawkes turned on his heel and started towards the door.

'Thousands of dollars,' Claire said softly. She leaned forward on her hands and smiled as the imposing form of her boss paused, then turned back. 'Thousands and thousands of dollars,' she repeated, 'while you hunt and hunt for someone, and work and work to train them. Have a nice year.'

Her boss essayed a scornful look. 'You're not irreplaceable.'

'I know,' Clare said with a regretful sigh. 'No one is. You will give me good references, won't you?' She picked up a bottle of aspirin and dropped it daintily into the bag. 'Maybe somewhere where I won't need those so often,' she mused aloud, pretending that she wasn't aware that Terrill Hawkes was studying her thoughtfully.

'All right, two weeks,' he said gruffly.

Claire flicked a glance at him and then stared down into the tote-bag while the silence stretched tight and thin as the rubber on a slingshot. Just as it seemed about to break, she nodded and looked up. 'All right. Two weeks,' she agreed.

Terrill Hawkes grimaced, shook his head, then turned and left the room, closing the door quietly behind him.

Frowning, Claire sat back down at her desk. It had been almost too easy. That last bit was definitely out of character. The door should have slammed. And was that slight droop to the shoulders a new wrinkle to play on her sympathies, or was the frantic pace of Terrill Hawkes finally catching up with him? She leaned forward and pressed a button as her intercom warbled.

'Yes, Jayne?' she answered.

'What was that little tête-à-tête all about?' enquired the soft voice of her secretary.

'Just negotiating my vacation,' Claire replied. 'Did Mr Hawkes look a little tired to you? He didn't seem quite up to par.'

'A little. All he said was "Grrmph," when I said good afternoon. Maybe it's got something to do with his farewell to Lady Millicent. By the way, did you pick up the bracelet for her?'

'Oh, lord,' Claire groaned, 'I forgot! I'll do it on my way home. But I doubt that discarding yet another rich, gorgeous, and this time titled lady has exhausted our great leader. Maybe he's only human and he's got a touch of the 'flu.'

'Could be. Did I hear the word Jamaica drifting softly through your door?'

'You did. That's my next assignment. I'll bring you down as soon as I have a look around.' Claire grinned to herself as Jayne gave a ladylike squeal.

'Terrific! I can hardly wait.'

'It won't be more than a month, I'd guess. Maybe less. Well, I'd better straighten up my desk and get out of here. Tell anyone who calls that I've already left, will you, please?'

'Yes, Miss Forsythe,' Jayne replied, her voice still sounding as if she were smiling over the prospect of going to Jamaica.

'If everyone in the world who wants to go to Jamaica went there at the same time the island would sink,' Claire muttered to herself as she began carefully removing the items from the tote-bag, discarding the fractured remnants of her coffee mug into the waste-paper basket. It was obviously a perfect place for Hawkes Hotels to establish its first resort outside the United States. She pulled a yellowed newspaper clipping from the bag, and brushed a few slivers of pottery from it, then looked at the picture and smiled.

It was a picture of herself standing next to Terrill Hawkes at the opening of the Las Vegas hotel and resort, Hawkes' Playground. That had been her very first job. Not just her first job with Terrill Hawkes, but the first job she had landed after she'd graduated from college, her degree in business administration in hand. What an incredible three years it had been since then! Not that it hadn't started out just as incredibly at Hawkes' Playground. If anyone had told her on the day that she first walked into the manager's office that she would have his job within a week, she would have told them they were crazy.

The problem with that poor man, she discovered later, had been that he thought he was supposed to manage a hotel, not oversee a complete renovation. When he found he was supposed to supervise everyone from architects to plumbers, and make dozens of unfamiliar decisions, he fell completely apart, thereby incurring the violent wrath of Terrill Hawkes, who had no tolerance for indecision. When the man apologised profusely, a fatal error when dealing with Mr Hawkes, he was fired on the spot, via long-distance. His assistant, a starched-looking woman named Beems, took his place. Claire had been hired as a lowly third assistant, her main task to oversee the accounts for the various contractors working on the renovation and make frequent reports on costs. She had just completed her first run-through and was about to present it to the new manager, when she heard loud voices coming from Ms Beems' office.

Claire smiled to herself at the memory. Her first introduction to Terrill Hawkes, the boy wonder of the hotel business, had been the sound of his voice roaring, 'What do you mean, can't? There is no such word in this organisation!'

'Really, Mr Hawkes,' Ms Beems' voice had replied loudly and shrilly, 'I think it's completely unrealistic to expect me to have such things done when all I have is an assistant fresh out of school. I'll be lucky to have her first report in a week. And I certainly have no intention of grovelling around to see if the plumbing is being done properly. That's the contractor's job, I believe.'

'And just who do you think is representing my interests?' Terrill Hawkes had asked thunderously, his words accompanied by a bang that Claire guessed must be the sound of his fist hitting the hapless Ms Beems' desk.

Exactly what had prompted her to knock on the door just then, Claire was never quite sure. Perhaps she was beginning to feel sorry for Ms Beems. Maybe it was the chance to produce her first report, long before Ms Beems thought she would. Or it could have been a desire to see Terrill Hawkes in person, something she hadn't really expected to do. She had seen his picture in various news magazines, usually a formal pose of him in his business clothes, sober-faced, with steely blue eyes and a grim set to his strong jaw. This was almost always accompanied by an older picture of him in his Chicago Bears' football uniform, with longish hair and a boyish grin on his ruggedly handsome face. Which one, she had wondered, was the real Terrill Hawkes?

Whatever her reason, Claire had straightened her shoulders beneath her trim, grey suit, given a pat to her neatly coiffed, ginger-coloured hair, which she wore pinned up in a smooth chignon, then raised her hand and knocked firmly on the door.

'Go away!' had come the snarl from Mr Hawkes. Claire had opened the door instead.

'I heard that you wanted the cost reports,' she said, accenting the "heard", and trying not to flinch as Terrill Hawkes stared her up and down with eyes that in real life were so blue that they seemed to gleam with an inner fire. Her first impression was that he was much bigger than she had imagined, and much better-looking. His dark hair was now cut fashionably short, and his black brows seemed almost to meet as he scowled at her.

'Who are you?' he demanded.

'Claire Forsythe, the fresh-out-of-school person,' she replied. 'The cost reports,' she added, holding out the folder of neat computer printouts, and feeling guilty as Terrill Hawkes turned his scowl on the unhappy Ms Beems and said sarcastically, 'Next week?' Her guilt was quickly alleviated when Ms Beems sniffed and gave her an unpleasant, sneering look.

'I doubt they'll be done right the first time,' she said, with a superior air that made Claire want to throw something at her.

'They are done perfectly correctly,' Claire said firmly, jerking her chin up and looking down her nose at Ms Beems. 'It was no problem at all once I had it set up on the computer.' There was no way in the world that she was about to admit that she had stayed up until the wee hours several nights getting it set up!

'They certainly appear to be,' Terrill Hawkes said, looking up from his perusal of them and then setting the folder down on the corner of Ms Beems' desk. He advanced on Claire and stopped just short of the point at which she would have considered retreat a good option. He cleared his throat and looked down at her very seriously.

'Miss Forsythe,' he said, 'how do you feel about plumbing? Is it beneath your notice?'

'No, sir,' she replied, tilting her head back to look up at the towering man. 'I especially notice when it doesn't work.'

'So do the guests in a hotel. Would you please inspect the work that is being done here and report back to me at, say, one o'clock tomorrow in this same office?'

For a brief moment, as those penetrating blue eyes, beneath brows that now arched upwards questioningly, stared into hers, Claire had an impulse to blurt out that she wouldn't know bad plumbing unless it jumped up and hit her. But something made her repress that response. Perhaps the way that Terrill Hawkes simply asked her to do the job, rather than ask her if she could, made her feel that she could do it. Perhaps something in the way those startlingly blue eyes looked so directly and unquestioningly into hers made her feel compelled to try. Whatever the reason, her answer was brief and affirmative.

'Certainly, Mr Hawkes,' she replied. 'Will that be all for now?'

'Yes, Miss Forsythe,' came the equally brief answer, followed by a dismissive little nod, and Claire had fled before the shards of ice flying from Ms Beems' angry glare could draw real blood.

It had taken Claire no more than a few moments to realise that she now had only a little more than twenty-four hours to do a job she hadn't the vaguest idea how to begin. She had seen plumbers working behind the swimming pool and in the new athletic facilities, but she couldn't very well walk up to them and simply say, 'How's it going?' She needed some quick information on what kinds of things to look for and ask about. Who could tell her what she needed to know? She went to a door and stared out into the brilliant desert sunshine, her mind whirling, tossing kaleidoscopic pieces into a merging plan. Within an hour she had her information.

She called the local plumbers' union and pretended to be a woman about to buy a home, needing to know how to tell if the plumbing was adequate and in good condition. They had both helpful tips and pamphlets for her. She found a do-it-yourself book on plumbing at a hardware store. Then, armed with a few facts and a winning smile, she began prowling the huge hotel, asking questions, and peering seriously at everything that was shown to her. By the time of her meeting with the formidable Mr Hawkes, she was convinced that the plumbing contractor was, in general, doing a good job, but was making some material substitutions that she thought might be inadequate. She reported the same, in detail, to Terrill Hawkes, who, in the absence of Ms Beems, was seated at Ms Beems' desk.

'Very good,' he said tersely, when she had finished. 'What did you do about it?'

The question struck Claire as strange, under the circumstances. 'Exactly what you told me to do,' she replied. 'I reported to you.'

'And exactly what does that contribute to solving the problem?' came the roar from a frowning Terrill Hawkes.

For a moment, Claire was taken aback at the roar and the frown. She had done nothing wrong. Then she put it together with what she had seen and heard the day before, and a kind of understanding clicked that had stood her in good stead ever since. Apparently, Mr Hawkes had his own, unique way of dealing with employees who were supposed to be in decision-making positions, a sort of football-style management technique. If she was now one of that group, he had failed to tell her about it. She didn't mind if he wanted to shout at her. She was used to holding her own in a family that did a lot of yelling and arm-waving. They, however, played fair. Mr Hawkes could learn right now that he couldn't put blame on her she didn't deserve, no matter how loudly he did it.

'Not much,' she replied, with a frown and a

presentable roar of her own, 'and if you want me to handle it I will. Just try to be more clear in the future. I can't read your mind.'

From the way Terrill Hawkes' blue eyes flashed at her response, Claire was afraid for a short time that she was about to be fired, and she set her jaw and glared back at the big man, ready to give him a piece of her mind for being so unreasonable. Instead, a few moments later he grinned, jumped to his feet, and gestured to the chair he had just vacated.

'Come and take your seat, Miss Forsythe,' he said. 'I do believe I have finally found me a manager. Ms Beems is no longer with us,' he added, as Claire stared at him, open-mouthed.

For the second time in as many days, Claire repressed a response which would have indicated that she felt totally unqualified to do the job she had been asked to do. 'You've got to be kidding,' was all she could think of, but she did not say it. Instead she walked slowly to the chair, sat down, and gratefully hid her shaking knees beneath the desk.

'Manager?' she said finally, when her new boss had taken a chair across the desk from her.

'That's right,' he replied. 'Not the usual hotel manager's job, of course. You are to manage the renovation. You are to be my eyes and ears when I'm not here, which will be most of the time, and to take care of any decisions which need to be made on the spot. Naturally, you should consult with me on anything major, but there should be very little of that. All of the details are worked out and documented, and what I want should be clear. The only remaining unfinished detail is the décor for the casino. I'll have some plans for that in a week or two. Any questions?'

*   *   *

Claire replaced the treasured old clipping in her desk drawer and shook her head, remembering. There had been so many questions that she felt dizzy, so instead of risking sounding like an idiot she had told Mr Hawkes that she wanted to study things first, before she asked. Then, when she did need to ask, he had been gone and she had had to make do on her own. The result had been some memorable shouting matches, as she defended her decisions and herself, a process which Terrill Hawkes seemed to thoroughly enjoy in a perverse sort of way. The 'You're fired, Miss Forsythe!' 'You can't fire me, Mr Hawkes, I quit!' routine alternated with, 'I quit!' 'Oh, no, you don't. You're fired!' as the inevitable conclusion to the tension that built between them when their opinions differed, as they frequently did. Sometimes they seemed to head straight for that sequence, like two actors in a long-running play, skipping to the all-too-familiar end.

It was, she often thought, as if that was the only way he knew how to relate to her, for their contacts aside from business were minimal and usually rather dull. Claire tried to make friends with the man, for she was naturally gregarious, but he was gruff and standoffish. For a time, this fascinated her, as did almost everything about her rich and famous boss. In fact, she readily admitted to herself later, she'd had a terrific crush on him for a while. But when they were not discussing business, he simply closed up.

She might have considered that a challenge, except that she quickly learned that he was not that way at all with many other women. The first lesson came when she arrived at her office in the Hawkes' Playground one morning to find Terrill Hawkes waiting for her in the company of one Marguerite McNally, the designer who was supposed to be doing the casino rooms, and who had insisted on dealing directly with Mr Hawkes. The fact that he had not objected should have given her a clue, Claire thought as she looked at the luscious redhead in the clinging satin jump-suit, and then took in with a sweeping glance the fact that her boss was wearing a sexy sweater instead of a jacket and tie, and his features seemed frozen into a permanent smile.

'I thought we'd run through some sketches and the specs with you,' Mr Hawkes said as soon as he had introduced Claire to Marguerite. 'Feel free to comment.'

Fortunately, Claire's intuition told her that the invitation to comment meant only positively, and so she murmured some polite inanities at what she saw, which seemed to her to be definitely uninspired design, very similar to several other places she had seen on the 'Strip', as the row of resort hotels and casinos in Las Vegas was known. At that early stage in their relationship, it was disappointing to her to find that Terrill Hawkes was falling victim to man's oldest infirmity, the inability to separate business from pleasure. Apparently, her disappointment had shown on her face, in spite of her efforts to hide it.

'You don't like it,' he had accused her as soon as Marguerite had departed. 'Let me remind you that your job is to see that the plans are executed, not to pass on your artistic opinion.'

'I didn't say one word about the design!' Claire had cried, trying to cover her failed neutrality with bluster.

'You didn't need to, Miss Forsythe. Your disapproval was obvious. Perhaps you aren't aware that Miss McNally is one of the best in the business.'

'What business?' Claire snapped back. It was
only milliseconds before she realised she should have
censored that last remark. Terrill Hawkes' black
brows met above the bridge of his nose.

'So,' he snarled, 'petty female jealousy is all it
takes to destroy your objectivity. What a pity! I had
thought better of you. I doubt I can even trust you to
see that the designs are carried out properly.'

Claire stared at him, glowering. She had probably
said more than enough already, but she was not
about to let him accuse her of faults that were his,
not hers. 'Believe me, Mr Hawkes,' she said with
icy calmness, 'I will be only too happy to see that
that tacky mess is executed just as it has been
designed. That will tell you who is objective and who
isn't, although that is a rather expensive way to
learn the lesson.'

'Are you accusing me of letting Miss McNally's
obvious charms cloud my judgement?' Terrill
Hawkes roared.

By that time, Claire was sure that her future with
Hawkes Hotels was limited to the next few minutes.
There was no point in backing down now.

'If the shoe fits!' she roared back.

Terrill Hawkes jumped to his feet from the chair
he had been occupying behind Claire's desk.

'Miss Forsythe, you're fired!' he thundered.

'Oh, no, I'm not!' she shouted. 'I quit!' She
turned and started towards the door with what she
hoped was a dignified bearing, her chin held high,
even though she felt her entire body shaking from
the intensity of their encounter. She had only got
half-way when Terrill Hawkes' voice, now sounding
quite normal, interrupted her.

'Miss Forsythe, come back here,' he said.

'What for?' Claire asked, turning and looking at him warily. He was sitting down again, tapping the ends of his fingers together and looking at her thoughtfully through narrowed eyes. He beckoned her closer.

'Perhaps we can reach an understanding,' he said. 'You don't try to interfere in my love-life, and I won't interfere with yours.'

Claire stared at him. Was that what he thought she was doing?

'I wasn't!' she cried. 'I wouldn't! I mean, I had no idea that Miss McNally was . . .' She stopped, suddenly aware that she was on the verge of making matters worse, and regathered her wits. 'The only thing I'm interested in is whether Miss McNally's designs are the best you could get for this hotel! I don't think they are.'

'Then why didn't you say so while we were looking at them? Miss McNally is a professional. She is used to criticism.'

'With you hovering over them like a giant Cheshire cat?'

The faintest suggestion of a smile flitted across Terrill Hawkes' rugged face. He stood up again, held out Claire's chair, and gestured for her to sit down. When she had done so, he silently proceeded towards the door, then stopped and turned back.

'Tacky? Just what did you mean by tacky?' he asked.

Claire gritted her teeth. If she wasn't really fired, she wished he would just shut up. 'Tacky,' she repeated, 'as in a plastic saguaro cactus with flashing lights for spines is tacky. Cheap-looking and not very original. There are dozens in town already.'

Terrill Hawkes nodded, whether in agreement or understanding, Claire could not tell. He reached for her door-handle, then looked back and gave her a raffish smile.

'Get to work, Miss Forsythe,' he said.

It took several more such encounters before Claire could get through them without her nerves being in a shambles afterwards although she soon learned to head off being fired by quitting as soon as Terrill Hawkes had got several good roars out of his system. Then it got to be more like a game, each of them playing for the most strategic time to make their pronouncement.

Claire never again commented on any of Terrill Hawkes' female friends, although she thought plenty of unflattering things about them. They all seemed to be tall, bosomy, and have totally vacant expressions. Whether that indicated blind adoration of the charismatic Terrill Hawkes, or just plain stupidity, she was never sure. The Hawkes groupies, she and Jayne called them behind his back. The only sign he gave that he appreciated her tact was that he began to give her the task of finding an appropriate 'farewell' gift for the ones he was discarding. Nor did he actually admit that was what he was doing, although it was obvious from the 'don't call me, I'll call you' kind of note he always wrote to accompany it, and the fact that Claire sometimes had to deal with frantic phone calls from the abandoned ladies.

From the long list of brief affairs, and a disastrous attempt to emulate one of that glamorous crew, Claire sadly concluded that Terrill Hawkes was simply not capable of, nor interested in, anything more than a superficial relationship with a woman.

It was at the opening of the Hawkes' Oasis in Palm Springs, only her second project for Terrill Hawkes, that Claire finally decided to try to get some response to her as a woman from him. Perhaps, she reasoned, it was because he had never seen her in anything but businesslike clothes that he was so gruff and unapproachable. There were plenty of elegant shops in Palm Springs, and a glittering crowd was expected for the opening, so she squandered a large sum on an especially chic and daring dress of champagne-coloured chiffon. Except for some floating panels, it clung like a second skin, and the back was cut to a V well below her waist. She let her ginger curls fly, and accented her large hazel eyes with shadow. There was no doubt in her mind that the dress had the desired effect, given the response of many of the men at the party. Terrill Hawkes, however, seemed not to notice, spending most of his time in amiable conversation with important guests.

After a glass of champagne to fortify her courage, Claire finally approached him when he was between conversations.

'Good evening, Mr Hawkes,' she said.

'Good evening, Miss Forsythe,' he replied, glancing at her briefly and then looking across the room.

Undaunted, Claire pressed on. 'Would you consider me too forward if I asked you to dance with me?'

'I don't dance,' he said gruffly, looking down at Claire and frowning. 'Old football injury.'

Claire made a *moue* and batted her eyelashes. 'What a pity. You're by far the handsomest man at this party.'

At that, Terrill Hawkes reached over and grasped Claire's wrist tightly in one of his huge hands.

'Come with me, Miss Forsythe,' he said, leading her from the grand ballroom so fast that she had to run to keep up. He took her into the manager's office and closed the door firmly behind them.

'Let me make something very clear to you, Miss Forsythe,' he growled. 'Our relationship is to be kept strictly business.'

'Let go of me,' Claire snapped, feeling her cheeks flaming, more in anger than embarrassment. 'How dare you assume I had . . . whatever you think I had in mind?'

Terrill Hawkes did not let go. He bent his head and glared menacingly at Claire. 'Because I know damned well what you had in mind! Look at that dress you're wearing! If that isn't a come-on, I don't know one when I see one!' His eyes executed a scathing circuit from Claire's face to her toes and back.

'It is not!' Claire hissed, not wanting to get the volume of their argument to a level where the guests at the party could hear. 'I simply wanted to look like a woman for a change, instead of some kind of humanoid robot that works her head off and gets yelled at for her trouble. What's wrong with you that you can't cope with that? Isn't there anything you recognise between something as sexless as a . . . a piece of furniture and a mistress?'

'I don't yell at the furniture,' he replied, 'nor do I pay it the kind of salary I pay you. If you want to keep drawing that salary, I suggest you look more like a piece of furniture in the future.'

'I will not!' Claire replied, enraged. The nerve of the man, thinking he could dictate what she would wear! She tried to jerk her wrist free again, but failed.

'Oh?' Terrill Hawkes' face was suddenly transformed by a seductive smile. 'Then perhaps you'd like to try for the other job you mentioned. It wouldn't last as long, but it could be a lot of fun. We'd start out something like this.'

With that, he pulled her into his arms, and his lips were on hers so quickly that Claire could only gasp before the shock sent her head to spinning. With consummate skill he teased her lips apart, the touch of his tongue sending icy hot tingles through her body that seemed to settle in her joints and turn them to jelly. Feeling as if she were sinking and swirling in space at the same time, Claire reached out to cling to Terrill Hawkes' broad back. When she did, his grasp loosened and his hands began to explore the bare expanse of her own back, insidiously creeping beneath the soft chiffon of her dress. One hand crept downwards, the other along the side, pushing her dress aside and baring her breast.

'Oh, don't,' Claire whimpered softly as his fingers teased the swollen peak. She was weak from surging currents of desire, unable to do anything except wait for that hand to move on where those currents led.

'Don't?' Terrill Hawkes murmured against her lips, while with one strong hand he pressed her against his hips. 'That's not what you're supposed to say.'

'Don't!' Claire cried, wrenching herself free, suddenly aware of what he meant. She pulled her dress back over her bare breast with trembling fingers, tears beginning to stream down her cheeks.

'You beast! What's wrong with you?'

Terrill Hawkes glared at her, his chest heaving. 'Don't persist in asking what's wrong with me,' he snarled. 'There is nothing wrong with me. What I have just demonstrated is exactly what I think women who dress like that are good for. I am not interested in marriage or companionship, and I never will be. If you want to add your name to the list of women who think they might persuade me to be interested in them for something besides sex, feel free. I don't think you'd do too badly. But you'd fail, just as all the rest will fail. Of course, I would have to fire you from your other job first. I don't mix business with pleasure.'

Claire was tempted to remind him of Marguerite McNally, but for once she held her tongue. She returned Terrill Hawkes' hard, cold glare with an intense stare of her own.

'No, thanks,' she said. 'If I wanted to be someone's mistress, which I don't, it certainly wouldn't be yours. There *is* something wrong with you. I don't know how you got to be the way you are, but it's a shame, it really is. The Terrill Hawkes who yells is a pretty nice guy. This one is a mess.' With that, she turned on her heel and left the room without a backward glance, ignoring a firm command that she put on a more modest dress.

She repaired her make-up and returned to the party, dancing the rest of the night away as if Terrill Hawkes did not exist. In the early morning hours she went to bed and had a good cry, not quite sure whether she was crying in disappointment, shame, or pity for the man whose warped view of women forever restricted him to such extremes of behaviour with them, forever prevented him from finding anything like love. She was curious about what event in his past might have produced his warped attitude. Was it the groupies who threw themselves at the handsome football star? Was it some bitter love-affair? She knew she would never find out from him, for he never spoke of his personal life, never asked about hers.

Nor did Terrill Hawkes ever mention their encounter that night. Claire might have thought she dreamed that kiss, except that she noticed a subtle shift in the pattern of their loud encounters. It was from that time on that they began to take on a more formal pattern, as if it were more an obligatory routine than a violent conflict. She wrote off her own interest in him as both hopeless and ridiculous, and filed it away under experience. When her busy life gave her time to go out with other men, she did so, but found she could not get very involved with any of them. Even though Terrill Hawkes was not the man for her, he was infinitely more exciting to be around than any other man. He treated her like an equal, was generous with praise when it was due, and paid her handsomely. She also discovered that his bluster hid a sensitive man, whose charitable works were legendary, and who could easily be taken advantage of by an unscrupulous person with a hard-luck story. She tried to protect him from them when she could, but often found it more tactful simply not to bother. He was so upset at finding that one poor injured workman was quite healthy enough to go dancing with one of the Las Vegas showgirls that he was unbearable company for days afterwards.

She sometimes wondered if she was missing something by not having any serious love interest, but she was so busy—four hotels renovated and one built from scratch in a little over three years—that she did not really care. She had become Terrill Hawkes' 'right-hand person', her title changed from manager of whatever project she was working on to executive co-ordinator, with a permanent office with her name and title on the door at the corporate headquarters in New York.

'And here I will probably be until I'm old and grey,' Claire mused as she tucked the last of the items from the tote-bag back into her desk. She sighed. Where would she rather be? Her salary was spectacular and she loved her work. Her parents, especially her mother, kept nagging that it was time for her to marry and settle down. They made it sound as if twenty-seven years old was one step short of senility. She would be spending the next two weeks listening to that.

Or . . . Claire tapped her chin thoughtfully with her forefinger . . . she could go to Jamaica and find her parents a nice spot at some resort not too close to Terrill Hawkes' villa, so that they could see each other but not be overwhelmingly close. That way, Mr Hawkes would think he had won after all, her parents would think she was extremely thoughtful, and the slight guilt she felt at having put the Jamaican project off would be alleviated. A wonderful idea!

Claire picked up her phone and dialled the Illinois number of her parents. In only a few minutes she had convinced them that a trip to Jamaica to see her would be far better than having her come to Illinois in the dead of winter, even though they would be unable to join her for another month.

'I have a research project to finish first,' her

father, a professor in the College of Agriculture and an expert on the breeding of cattle, told her. 'I'd enjoy going to Montego Bay, though. One of my former students, Harold Hanover, works for a crusty old fellow named Ben Williams who has a large cattle ranch somewhere near there. I met him at a conference in Kingston a year or so ago.'

'I'll find out where they are so you can look them up,' Claire promised.

'I may have a telephone number for Harold,' Roger Forsythe said. 'Hang on. I'll go and look.'

While he did, Claire listened patiently to her mother's cluckings about Claire staying with Terrill Hawkes at his villa.

'It just doesn't look right,' she complained. 'Wasn't that where you said he takes all of those fancy women of his?'

'No, Mother. He doesn't take them there. In fact, he never goes there himself. He bought the villa years ago when he was still a football player, but since he's been in the hotel business it's only been used as a place for the corporate executives to take their families. I'm not even sure he'll be staying there this time. And even if he does, there's nothing illicit going on between us. We don't even call each other by first names,' she explained, although she knew nothing would persuade her mother that her eldest daughter was not living a life of sin. She had frequently told Claire that 'everyone knew' that the only women who didn't prefer marriage to a career were the ones who were having wild affairs with their bosses.

'Your mother's an anachronism,' her father said when he came back on the line and Claire complained of her mother's misconceptions.

'I think it's those soap operas she watches,' Claire said, 'where everyone's carrying on with someone they aren't married to.' She wrote down the name and number of her father's former student, promising faithfully to call and tell him that her father would be coming.

That done, she told her surprised secretary to cancel her reservations to Illinois and book her a flight to Jamaica on the morrow, and went to give Terrill Hawkes his moment of triumph.

'So! You actually felt guilty at leaving me in the lurch,' he gloated.

'Not at all,' Claire retorted. 'I suddenly realised my choice was between being cold in Illinois or warm in Jamaica. I called my parents and told them I'd find them a lovely spot at a resort down there for two weeks. At your expense.'

Terrill Hawkes opened his mouth as if he were about to speak, and then closed it again, frowning.

'What?' Claire asked. It was unlike him to keep quiet about anything, especially something like getting stuck with a large bill.

'Nothing. I was going to suggest they might stay at the villa. There's plenty of room, but this might not be a good time for them to be there. Go ahead, get them a spot somewhere nearby. There are some nice spots at Doctor's Cave Beach, as I recall.'

That was curious, Claire thought. What might make it a bad time? Was he planning on bringing one of his lady-friends along when he came down? If he was, she'd move out herself, in a hurry. She wasn't about to hang around and watch one of his affairs first-hand! But all she said was, 'They can't come down for a month yet, but I wouldn't want them at the villa anyhow. Daddy's fine, but my mother tends to nag. Well, I'll be off tomorrow. Have you any words of wisdom for me before I go?'

'Nothing special, I guess,' he said rather diffidently. 'Let's see.' He rummaged around on his disorderly desk-top. 'Here,' he said finally, handing a slick, colourful brochure to Claire. 'This is the way the place looked under the previous owner. As you can see, it's five two-storey buildings radiating from a central courtyard and pool. I thought we'd call it Hawkes' Jamaican Star, and I want it to be the most beautiful hotel in all of Jamaica, so you can do your planning from that viewpoint. Aside from that, I haven't put much thought into it yet.'

'My planning?' Claire glanced at the brochure and then looked at Terrill Hawkes questioningly. Usually he had a million ideas of his own, his fertile mind moving a mile a minute and his comments keeping pace. Now he wanted her to turn some derelict buidings into the most beautiful hotel in Jamaica? 'Aren't you coming down to Jamaica yourself?'

'Oh, yes. In a week or so. I have to go to Rochester to see . . . a certain person, but then I'll be there to stay for quite a while. Don't worry,' he added with a knowing look as Claire glanced at him sharply, 'I'm not bringing anyone with me.'

'The thought never entered my mind,' she replied. 'I was just reminded that I need a note from you to Lady Millicent to go with that bracelet I'm going to pick up on my way home. I could probably write it myself, but she might wonder about the handwriting.'

'Oh, yes.' Terrill Hawkes flicked her an amused glance and picked up another sheet of paper, quickly scrawling a short note. 'There you are. Could you have written that one?'

Claire glanced at the note and then tucked it into her bag, a wry little smile flitting across her face. No, this one was different. Apparently, even Terrill Hawkes didn't win them all. Instead of the familiar, 'In memory of all the good times we shared,' it said, 'Congratulations. I hope you and Kevin will be very happy.'

'No, I guess I couldn't,' she replied. She raised her eyebrows at the knowing quirk of her boss's lips. 'Is something entertaining you?'

'Not exactly. I was just noticing that evil little smile of yours. You don't approve of my note? I should have thought you'd be pleased.'

'Pleased?' Claire said tightly. 'Why should I be pleased that you struck out with Lady Millicent?'

'Oh, so that's what you think.' Terrill Hawkes grinned broadly. 'Actually, I had no designs at all upon her ladyship. I introduced her to a friend of mine, Kevin Vandermeer, and I am sincerely glad that they hit it off so well. They plan to be married in June.'

'That's very nice,' Claire said, wishing that Terrill Hawkes would drop the subject. It made her very uncomfortable.

'You don't approve of my love-life, do you?' he asked, persevering upon that forbidden topic.

'Mr Hawkes,' Claire replied, becoming louder in exasperation, 'you told me some time ago not to interfere in your love-life. Therefore, I neither approve nor disapprove.'

'You don't approve.' Terrill Hawkes said it firmly this time.

Why, Claire wondered, was he choosing this time to open up a subject that he had declared closed so long ago? She would dearly love to tell him what she thought of both his choice of women and his frequent, short-lived, shallow affairs, but this did not seem like a good time to open that particular can of worms.

'Can we just drop the subject?' she said. 'If I have any opinion, it is private.'

Terrill Hawkes snorted. 'That's a ridiculous statement, given the fact that your opinion shows quite clearly on your face.'

'Then why ask?' Claire snapped. 'You obviously don't give a darn, since I seriously doubt this is the first time you've guessed what it was.'

'Why, Miss Forsythe,' Terrill Hawkes tried to look wounded, 'you know how much I value your opinion.'

For a moment, Claire was tempted to give him that opinion in vivid detail, but then she shook her head. 'Oh, no, you don't,' she said. 'I'm not biting on that one. If I really told you what I think, you'd probably fire me for real.'

'That bad?'

'Yes, that bad,' Claire said, nodding. 'Now, if you're through, I'd better be going, or the jewellers will be closed.'

Terrill Hawkes glanced at his watch. 'No, they won't. Miss Forsythe, do you think I'm too old to reform?'

Claire blinked, taken aback, mystified as to why her opinion was so suddenly being sought, when for years Terrill Hawkes had studiously avoided discussing anything very personal. Was he really about to turn over a new leaf? It was certainly past time he did. Maybe it had something to do with that 'certain person' he was going to see.

'Certainly not,' she replied. 'Thirty-five isn't old.'

'Thank you.' He gave a dismissive little nod, and Claire turned to go. 'Er—one other thing, Miss Forsythe,' he said.

Claire paused. 'Yes?' she said impatiently. At this rate, the shop *would* be closed!

'You'll find that things in Jamaica don't move at quite the same pace as they do here, so just relax and get used to moving at Jamaican speed. Don't try to get everything underway before I get there.'

'But you said . . .' Claire began, then stopped as Terrill Hawkes responded to an important incoming call. What on earth was going on? First he acted as if her getting to Jamaica at top speed was a matter of life and death, and then he told her to relax. He never told anyone to relax! Obviously she wasn't going to find out now, for he turned his attention to the call and gave her a silent goodbye salute.

'See you later,' she said softly. 'Take care.' With that, she went on her way, still meditating over both his unusual choice of words and his unusual concern with her opinion about his love-life. Just what did he mean by reform, and how relaxed could she be before he pounced on her like an enraged tiger and accused her of being lazy? Both made her feel strangely on edge, and quite relieved that she had decided to go to Jamaica immediately, after all. Something was going on with Terrill Hawkes that she did not know about, and she was dying to find out what it was.

CHAPTER TWO

CLAIRE stared out of the window as the plane began to reduce altitude approaching Montego Bay.

'It really *is* that colour!' she said excitedly, turning to the beautiful Jamaican woman sitting next to her.

'The sea?' The woman smiled as Claire nodded. 'Cerulean blue. Yes, it is lovely, isn't it? And the temperature of the water is in the low seventies. Perfect for swimming.'

'Oooh!' Claire shook her head in amazement. 'I'm afraid I always thought they did something to the photographs to make it look that way. It's incredibly lovely.'

As the plane dropped lower she could see reefs, turning the sea into pools varying in colour from pale blue to deepest midnight. A few white sails flashed brightly in the sunshine. She had only a brief glimpse of a bit of green island, and then they were on the ground. Stepping off the plane, clutching the heavy winter coat she had needed in snowy New York only hours before, she felt the warm tropical sun on her shoulders and was more pleased than ever that she had chosen Jamaica over Illinois in mid-winter. In a short while she had cleared her bags through Customs, exchanged some of her money for Jamaican dollars, and mounted the stairs to the reception area. She had called the villa to confirm her arrival time, and had been told that Mr

Hawkes' driver, Ernest, would meet her and would recognise her, but in the waiting throng she wondered how that would be possible. She stood still, looking around her at the crowd in their brightly coloured summer clothing. Her eye was caught by a towering, muscular Jamaican, who was purposefully scanning the new arrivals. Immediately he smiled broadly and approached her.

'Welcome to Jamaica, Miss Forsythe,' he said. 'My name is Ernest. I will take charge of your baggage now. And your coat, too. You will not need it here.'

'Thank you, Ernest,' Claire said, handing over her things. 'How on earth did you recognise me?'

'Mr Hawkes gave a very good description,' Ernest replied.

Claire followed Ernest through a shaded *lanai* and out to the car park, wondering how Terrill Hawkes might have described her to Ernest. What had he said about her? Look for a medium-size woman with ginger-coloured hair and an anxious expression?

They stopped by a shiny mini-van, and Ernest helped Claire into the front seat and then loaded her luggage into the back.

'I drive tour groups around the island when none of Mr Hawkes' employees are here,' Ernest explained as he got in, 'and when the villa has many guests, I take them wherever they want to go. I know all of the history of the island, all about the plants and animals, and all of the best places to go for recreation and dining. If there is anything you want to see, I am at your disposal. Mr Hawkes keeps a small car here for guests who wish to drive themselves, but you will find it much easier to let me take you than trying to drive yourself in the unfamiliar traffic.'

'I see,' Claire said thoughtfully. 'And no doubt you will be a great help in finding other good tour drivers for the guests at Mr Hawkes' new hotel?'

'Oh, yes, I shall know who to recommend,' Ernest replied cheerfully, confirming Claire's suspicion that at least that detail was already well in hand. 'Look there,' Ernest said, gesturing to his left as they began to move slowly with the traffic. 'We are about to run over a sleeping policeman.'

'A what?' Claire looked around, startled, then laughed as she saw a sign warning, 'Caution, Sleeping Policeman', and discovered that it was a large bump in the road, guaranteed to slow the traffic. 'We call them traffic bumps back home,' she said. 'How very unimaginative we are.'

'The villa is a short distance west and then up in the hills,' Ernest said as they left the airport complex. 'The property Mr Hawkes has just purchased is a few miles east of the airport. He said to take you there any time you were ready to look it over, but I think you will probably want to wait until the morning. That will give you time to get settled in and rest from your trip.'

'Yes . . . I think morning would be better,' Claire replied. Back in the States she would have dropped her baggage in her room and gone tearing off to inspect the new property, but already she was falling under the spell of this tropical land, her head swivelling rapidly to take in the sights between gasps at what she feared were imminent collisions. It was strange enough to be driving on the left side of the road, but Ernest's technique of honking and then passing other cars in spaces that seemed entirely too small, but which seemed to expand magically in response to his persistent horn, was positively heart-stopping. No wonder he had offered to do the driving. Not only would Mr Hawkes' doubtless expensive car be in jeopardy, but she definitely would be at a loss to drive with anything approaching Ernest's panache!

Between moments of seat clutching, Claire recognised bougainvillaea vines in lush and spectacular shades of red and purple growing on cottage walls near the cerulean sea, but a tree which looked as if someone had climbed into its branches and festooned it with huge bouquets of orange-red flowers was unfamiliar.

'Poinciana,' Ernest identified it.

In small, grassy spots, cattle grazed in amiable companionship with snowy egrets riding along on their backs.

'They are good friends. The birds eat the insects that bother the cattle,' Ernest explained.

'How my father will love that!' Claire exclaimed. She told Ernest about her father's profession and her parents' imminent visit to the island. 'Perhaps you could recommend a place for them to stay? Mr Hawkes suggested some place called Doctor's Cave Beach.'

'There are some nice places there. I will make some enquiries and take you there tomorrow. It is the busy season, but for a guest of Mr Hawkes, I am sure something will be available.'

Money talks, Claire thought wryly. Well, as long as it was Terrill Hawkes' money, she didn't mind. He had more than enough.

Ernest leaned heavily on the horn again, then lurched sharply to his left and started up a steep hill. The van passed several colourful small houses as it climbed higher. Then it turned left again between two concrete pillars with lanterns on the tops, climbed an even steeper hill, and came to a stop at the top before a sprawling white house with pointed, red-tiled roofs over each of its several wings.

'Welcome to Paradise,' Ernest said as he opened the door for Claire. 'That is what Mr Hawkes has named his house, and it truly is that.'

Claire got out and moved as if in a dream past beds of multicoloured crotons—immense, healthy-looking versions of the scrawny ones she had tried to grow in pots at home. A wrought-iron gate opened into an atrium with more crotons and bright begonias. At the heavy oaken door at the end of the atrium stood a smiling Jamaican woman in a trim blue uniform with a bright scarf around her head.

'Welcome, Miss Forsythe. I am Marisa, Mr Hawkes' housekeeper. I hope you had a pleasant trip?'

'Very nice, but the end is by far the best part,' Claire replied.

'Would you like to change into something more comfortable, and then have a drink of tropical punch on the patio before dinner?' Marisa enquired.

'That sounds lovely,' Claire agreed. She followed as Marisa led her through a covered *lanai* where a bowl of hibiscus blooms decorated a glass-topped dining-table, then paused, entranced. A few steps down from a covered balcony that ran along the length of the seaview side of the main section of the house, was a large patio surrounding a swimming pool, an iron railing protecting sun-worshippers and party-goers from plummeting down the steep hillside beyond. In the distance was a spectacular view of the entire harbour at Montego Bay, a huge white cruise ship just pulling in to dock. When she recovered from her trance to accompany Marisa to the bedroom wing at the far end of the balcony, she found that her bedroom windows opened on to the same entrancing scene.

A housemaid was already unpacking her things, and Claire quickly picked out a colourful print shirt and some shorts and sandals. This was going to be more like a vacation than work! The only question was, how was she ever going to get anything done? For as soon as she stretched out in the lounge chair on the patio and felt the warmth of the sun on her pale, bare arms and legs, she couldn't imagine ever wanting to move again. Well, Terrill Hawkes had told her to relax, hadn't he? At least for the rest of this day, she was going to take his advice. Tomorrow would be soon enough to begin figuring out how to carry out Terrill Hawkes' demands for the most beautiful hotel in Jamaica. Her perusal of the brochures for the former Melrose Beach hotel told her it was going to be a very big job.

In the morning, Claire wandered through the villa, sipping on her third cup of coffee and still feeling a little groggy. A surprising array of night sounds had made it difficult to fall asleep.

'There are many, many houses in the hills behind us, and every one has several dogs and at least one donkey,' Marisa had explained. 'At night, the animals all talk to each other about their people. You will quickly grow used to them.'

'I rather liked it, but it was a shock,' Claire said. 'I thought we were all alone on this mountain top. It took me a while to figure out that that terrible wheezing sound was donkeys braying.'

Terrill Hawkes' Paradise was indeed spacious and lovely, but to Claire's eye it seemed a bit austere, and some of the furnishings were worn and walls needed repainting. The colours were too drab for her taste, too, and the area rugs that were scattered on the gleaming tiled floors were a disaster. They looked like chunks cut from a roll of brown shag carpeting, and refused to lie flat. The piece by her bed had tripped her up once already. All in all, it wasn't up to Terrill Hawkes' usual standards. She recalled hearing that he had bought it furnished from the previous owner. Strange that he hadn't had it redecorated in all that time. But maybe it had suited him before he started buying hotels. However . . . she smiled wryly at the thought . . . he could at least have had Marguerite McNally come down and install a few lighted cacti to brighten things up!

'Mr Hawkes is on the telephone for you,' Marisa announced, locating Claire in the large living-room. 'You can take the call in the office. Just follow the hall left from the balcony. It is the last door on the right.'

The office was a bare little room, with a large oak desk, a typewriter, and bookshelves which contained a few piles of old magazines. Apparently it was here for those visiting executives who just couldn't stop working, even in Jamaica. Well, it would doubtless look quite different when Terrill Hawkes got this latest project underway.

'Hello, Mr Hawkes,' she said, sitting down at the desk and picking up the receiver.

'Hello, Miss Forsythe. How are things in Paradise?'

'Marvellous,' she replied. 'I think I could easily become very lazy here. But I plan to have Ernest take me to the new property at ten o'clock. That should wake me up and get my mind working again. Is there something you forgot to tell me about? We didn't have much time to discuss it before I left.'

'No. I just wanted to be sure you got there all right and that everything was in order. How is the weather?'

'Oh, it's . . . perfect,' Claire replied, puzzled. Terrill Hawkes never wasted time talking about the weather.

'Good,' he said, pursuing the topic. 'There's a lot of snow here.'

Here. It occurred to Claire that he must be in Rochester now, but that she did not know whether it was Rochester, New York, or Rochester, Minnesota. Either one might be snowy. 'I can imagine,' she replied. 'Uh, how are things in Rochester?' she asked, hoping for a clue.

'I'm about to find out,' he replied, while in the background Claire heard the sound of someone being paged over a loudspeaker. He must be at the airport, waiting to be picked up by that 'certain person'.

'Well, have a good time,' she said.

There was a short pause, and Claire heard Terrill Hawkes saying to someone, 'I'll be right there.'

'I've got to go now,' he said to her. 'Don't get too sunburned.'

Claire frowned. Now he was worried about her getting sunburned? 'I—I won't,' she replied. 'I'll be careful.'

'Good. I expect I'll be there by next Monday.'

'Fine,' Claire replied. 'I should have a lot to report on by then.'

'Don't work too hard. Have Ernest take you to see

some of the sights.'

A sense of unreality began to creep into Claire's consciousness. Terrill Hawkes never told anyone not to work too hard! At first she could think of no reply, at last stammering out, 'All right, if you say so.'

'I do. Goodbye—er—Miss Forsythe.'

'Goodbye, Mr Hawkes. I'll see you next Monday.'

Claire frowned and dropped the receiver into its cradle, her uneasiness of the previous day returning, magnified several-fold. Her intuition that Terrill Hawkes was undergoing some kind of a change had certainly been on the mark. That had been the most uninformative conversation she had ever had with him. Why had he called at all? Just to warn her not to get sunburned or to work too hard? She shook her head and sighed. There was no use trying to figure it out until he got here in person. Maybe then she could get some answers from him.

'I see you have decided to adopt the tourist fashions,' Ernest said approvingly when, promptly at ten o'clock, he arrived to take Claire to see the new property. She had again put on a loose shirt and shorts, and tied her hair into a ponytail rather than pin it into a tight topknot.

'I'd feel a little silly here in a business suit,' Claire replied with a grin.

'You should have a straw hat. The sun is quite treacherous to the unaccustomed,' Ernest said. 'I shall stop so that you can buy one.'

'Good idea,' Claire agreed, and when they had retraced their trip of the day before almost to town, Ernest let her out at an open-air market, where native craftsmen displayed their wares. In a few minutes she had picked out a wide-brimmed hat, embroidered with straw flowers in bright orange and yellow.

'Now you will be safe from the sun,' Ernest told her. 'We shall stop next at the hotel where your parents may stay, so that you can see if you approve. It is right on the beach, and there is good food and shopping all around.'

'My mother will love the shopping and my father will love the food,' Claire said. She found the place exactly right for her parents, comfortable but not too ostentatious. Her father, she knew, would hate any place where all the guests looked as if they drove Mercedes back home. He might be one of the world's most famous animal geneticists, but he still thought of himself as a farm boy from Illinois.

After leaving the quiet street near the hotel, Ernest eased back into the flow of traffic, blasting away on his horn, and soon Claire recognised the turn to the airport. They went past it, along the highway heading east, Ernest chatting informatively as they went about the other hotels, the sugar-cane fields they passed, and the assorted unfamiliar trees that fascinated Claire, which included everything from a Norfolk pine grown to a towering height, to breadfruit trees with their wide, fan-shaped leaves.

'There should be no trouble having beautifully landscaped grounds here,' Claire commented.

'Like everything else, it only requires attention,' Ernest said with a sigh, leading Claire to expect that the grounds she was about to see were in sorry shape.

In a few minutes she found that her guess was right. The first clue was the broken-down entrance gate, a tattered sign announcing the 'OSE BEACH

RESO', and a guard who saluted Ernest as they passed through.

'Mr Hawkes finally hired security people to keep trespassers out,' Ernest told Claire when she asked. 'Beachcombers and ruffians have broken many windows. Such things happen when a place is neglected.'

'Naturally,' Claire agreed, her critical eye taking in the remnants of once attractive gardens alongside the drive which they now followed towards the sea. 'Why did the hotel fail, do you know? It seems a perfect spot, fairly close to the town, but quiet.'

'A lazy manager and an owner who paid no heed,' Ernest replied succinctly. 'No one will stay where the food is bad and the service is terrible.' He gave Claire a sideways glance. 'And, of course, there was the rumour of a ghost who walked the beach at night. It made some people nervous.'

'A ghost on the beach?' Claire raised her eyebrows at Ernest. 'Are you serious?'

'Oh, yes, ma'am,' Ernest replied. 'I don't believe in such things myself, of course, but many people do. There are many legends of ghosts here. A very famous one inhabits the old mansion known as the Greenwood Greathouse. And there is the legend of a ghostly witch at the Rose Hall mansion. They are a great tourist attraction. One more does not surprise people. Perhaps, they said, it was someone lost at sea.'

'Oh, my!' Claire said, shivering involuntarily. When Ernest gave her a knowing look, she smiled quickly. 'I don't really believe in ghosts, either, but ghost stories always set me tingling in a funny sort of way. Well, I guess we'll have to either turn our ghost into a tourist attraction too, or else have floodlights on the beach to keep it away.'

Ernest nodded. 'There,' he said, slowing the van at a point where the land began sloping towards the sea. 'Now you can see the buildings ahead and the sea beyond. The beach is below, down a small cliff at that end . . .' He gestured towards the west. 'There are steps cut into the rocks. That makes it very private.' He stopped the van so that Claire could look at the hotel as arriving guests would first see it.

'From here, it looks very inviting,' Claire said.

'The centre building on the far side had the reception area. It's in the worst condition. There was a fire there after the hotel was abandoned, and at one time a family had moved in with some goats.'

'Oh, my!' Claire said. 'I never had to cope with goats in the lobby before.' She frowned as a thought suddenly struck her, 'How long has this place been for sale?'

'It was not for sale for very long. Mr Hawkes bought it as soon as I notified him that it was for sale. That was almost three years ago.'

'Three years ago?' Claire's voice squeaked in surprise. Of all the strange things she had heard in the past two days, that was the topper!

'Yes,' Ernest went on, 'many years ago, before the hotel was built, Mr Hawkes tried to buy this property. That was before I worked for him. He left word that if it were ever to come up for sale, he should be notified immediately. I know many people, and I heard rumours, so I gave him the information. At first Mr Hawkes did not seem interested in putting the hotel back in working order. Too much work in the States, he said. I am glad he is finally going to do so. It will give work to many people.'

'Yes, that is good,' Claire murmured, while her mind was in a whirl, trying to comprehend this new and bizarre twist. It almost seemed she might have dreamed that only two days ago Terrill Hawkes had said he'd 'finally found' the property he'd been looking for, and had roared on about losing money almost every minute it stood empty. The only reasonable explanation she could come up with was that there might have been some problem about title to the property that had just been resolved, and that the story he gave her was a clever ploy to make everything look crucial so that she'd abandon her trip home. That would certainly be in character for him. But it wouldn't be in character at all for him not to have had any ideas about what he wanted done, nor to have told her about it before. Three years? She couldn't recall him having made a trip to Jamaica at that time, but, of course, she didn't keep track of all of his comings and goings. Still, he usually told her where he could be reached. She turned to Ernest.

'Could it have been more than three years ago when Mr Hawkes bought the hotel?' she asked. If it had happened before she went to work for Terrill Hawkes, that might explain her not knowing.

'No, Miss Forsythe,' Ernest replied. 'It was exactly three years ago next month. I remember, because it was on my cousin's birthday. Mr Hawkes flew down and signed the papers, then left again immediately. He was too busy to even go to inspect the property.' He smiled proudly. 'He had asked me to be his agent and certify that it was as represented. I have looked after it for him ever since.'

'I see,' Claire said, although she did not see at all. 'Well, let's go on. I guess it's time I started figuring out what needs to be done.'

For several hours Claire roamed the buildings, quickly reaching the conclusion that the previous owner had had reasonably good builders, but had also cut every corner he could. The plumbing fixtures were cheap and atrocious, the furnishings no better. There were too many small rooms. Walls would have to be moved, rooms joined to make suites, if it were to be a luxury hotel. It would require a creative architect to make something spectacular out of the rather plain buildings.

'It will take a lot of work,' Claire said, detailing some of her findings to Ernest, who had followed her on her rounds. 'Mr Hawkes has an architect he usually works with in the States, but I'd rather find someone here, if possible. Do you know who I might contact about finding one?'

'Oh, yes,' Ernest replied. 'I have several relatives in the building trades. My brother and his sons do electrical work, my cousin is the best carpenter in Jamaica, and he has several men who work for him. They will know who to recommend.'

'Excellent,' Claire said, nodding. If Terrill Hawkes trusted Ernest to be his agent, she was sure she could trust him, too. 'And now,' she said, as they began walking around the grounds, 'tell me if you have any relatives in the landscape business.'

Ernest grinned. 'No, but I have a friend who is.'

'Send him around,' Claire said. 'We might as well begin . . . Oh, for goodness' sake, look at that!' Just ahead of them were three large, red cattle, happily grazing by the tennis courts.

'They are from the ranch next door,' Ernest said, his expression angry. 'The man will not fix his fence. I shoo them back all the time, but when I call he only curses at me.'

'Well, let's shoo them back again, and then go and have a talk with the man,' Claire said. 'If he curses at me I'll give him a piece of my mind.' She took off her hat and waved it. 'Come on, girls, let's move it! Back home,' she said.

'You work with your father's cattle?' Ernest asked, when the three cows had calmly trotted back through a large gap in a dilapidated fence.

'Lots, when we lived on a farm,' Claire replied. They twisted the broken wires together as best they could. 'Now,' she said, 'let's go and see this sloppy rancher. This fence is a disgrace. What's his name?'

'Williams,' Ernest replied. 'But I think maybe you shouldn't go right in to see him. He is a most unpleasant man.'

'Ben Williams?' Claire asked, remembering the name her father had mentioned.

Ernest nodded.

'Then he knows my father. Perhaps that will keep him from cursing at me. One of my father's former students works for him, too. If he's rude, I'll tell my father. Maybe he'll be able to straighten things out.'

'I don't know,' Ernest said, looking apprehensive. 'I never hear of anyone who can get along with Mr Williams. But if you insist . . .'

'I do,' Claire said firmly. There wouldn't be much point in starting to landscape the grounds if herds of cattle were going to be wandering in and out. As they drove away, she said thoughtfully, 'You know, I might even ask Mr Williams to sell us a strip of land so we could plant a shelter of trees along this side.'

Ernest only shook his head, his expression even more distressed.

It was a long drive to the ranch entrance, and Claire noticed the rest of the fence they passed was in good repair. It was almost as if Mr Williams wanted his cattle to graze on the hotel grounds.

They drove past several well-kept barns and pens. Then the road turned bumpy and followed a row of sick-looking palm trees around a small hill. The drive ended some fifty yards from the house. It was a magnificent house, long and low, clinging to the edge of a cliff above the sea, but it had an air of loneliness that was almost oppressive. The windows were shuttered, the yard unkempt, and the umbrella over a table on a low-walled terrace was tattered from the winds.

'Are you sure this is where Mr Williams lives?' Claire asked, turning towards Ernest. 'It doesn't look as if anyone lives here.'

'Yes, ma'am,' Ernest replied. 'He is a strange man. No one comes to see him. He goes to see those he wishes to see. I think maybe it would be better if you were to phone.'

'Maybe,' Claire replied grimly, 'but as long as we're here, I'll give it a try.' She got out of the van and began walking up the little-used path towards the door, feeling an uneasy quivering in her stomach as she approached the dark, lonely house. Perhaps Ernest was right, she thought, then scolded herself for letting his earlier talk of ghosts make her nervous. But still, if the man was a recluse of some sort, she might be making a mistake . . .

She was sure of it as soon as she had knocked on the door and saw the dour, leathery face of Ben Williams.

'What do you want?' he snarled.

Claire had no sooner given her name, mentioned

the cattle, and said she was a representative of Hawkes Hotels when he loosed a stream of profanity, his eyes wild and bright.

'Get off of my property!' he yelled, when Claire stood staring at him, shocked. 'Don't ever come near here! And tell that devil Hawkes I don't want him or his hotel anywhere near here, either. The man is a son of Satan! And if he thinks a few cattle are trouble, he hasn't seen anything yet. Now get the hell off of my property and stay off! Anyone that gets near Hawkes is touched by his evil.' He glared at Claire, one arm raised menacingly. 'Go!'

Evil? Claire could not imagine what Terrill Hawkes could have done to incur such hatred. She felt temper begin to simmer at this man's unreasonable accusations.

'I'm going,' she said hastily, when Williams made a move towards her. 'But I'm not going to put up with your blasted cattle on the hotel grounds, that's for sure! Next time they come visiting, I'll keep them until you fix your fence.'

Ben Williams sneered. 'You can't do that. You don't know anything about cattle.'

'Oh, no?' Claire stuck out her chin and glared back at the man from a safe distance. 'My father is Roger Forsythe, and I know plenty about cattle. If any more of yours come visiting, I'll herd them into the tennis courts and keep them there, under armed guards if necessary, until you fix your fence!' With that, she turned and stalked away.

She got into the van and slammed the door behind her, shaking her head at Ernest's questioning look. 'No luck,' she said. 'The man's half crazed when you mention Mr Hawkes.'

She looked back at the house. Ben Williams had

disappeared again, leaving the place looking as deserted as before.

'Let's go,' said Claire, shivering suddenly and looking at Ernest. 'There's something spooky about this place.'

'Yes, ma'am,' Ernest agreed, accelerating away rapidly in a cloud of dust.

For the next few days Claire tried to put her visit to the unpleasant Ben Williams out of her mind, but could not. She was curious about why he hated Terrill Hawkes, but it was more than that, she finally decided. It was the fact that he had called him evil, a son of Satan, epithets that were redolent with the supernatural. It reminded her of the voodoo religion prevalent on other Caribbean islands, and of ghosts that wandered beaches and ancient mansions. Could the man believe that Terrill Hawkes had cast some kind of spell on him? A call to Harold Hanover, her father's former pupil, did nothing to solve the mystery. Williams had shut himself up in his house since his daughter had drowned many years before, but when he ventured out to his cattle barns he seemed perfectly reasonable, if somewhat short-tempered. Harold was sure he would be happy to see Roger Forsythe, although not at his house. All Claire could hope then was that Terrill Hawkes could shed some light on the problem when he arrived.

The rest of the time, Claire had a first meeting with the young architect Ernest's brother recommended, and met several of Ernest's other industrious relatives. Together they figured out how to turn the tennis courts into a temporary cattle pen if any more of Williams' cattle wandered on to the property. But none did, the fence having been mysteriously repaired one night with new, sturdy wire. Apparently, Claire thought wryly, Ben Williams didn't want his precious cattle touched by Terrill Hawkes' evil, either.

After that, Claire relaxed as she had been instructed, and took progressively longer naps by the pool as her tan deepened. Jamaican speed, she mused, was exactly her speed. Marisa and Ernest persuaded her to take a trip to the beautiful white sand beach at Negril on Sunday, where she sampled some native cooking in a thatch-roofed, open-air restaurant by the shore, and had her hair done in an intricate set of braids at an impromptu beauty salon set up on the beach by several Jamaican girls.

On Monday morning she made a hurried trip to the hotel for a conference with the architect, and to ready herself for a report to Terrill Hawkes, who, she was sure, would not be nearly as relaxed as she had been when he arrived later that day. No leopard could change his spots overnight.

It was shortly after noon when Ernest returned Claire to the villa. Marisa appeared at the door as soon as the van drew up in front.

'Mr Hawkes has arrived,' she announced, with such a ceremonious air that Claire almost expected several uniformed trumpeters to materialise behind her and blow a fanfare, after which she would be escorted to meet the great man sitting upon a throne. 'He wanted to see you as soon as you returned.'

'Thank you, Marisa,' Claire replied, thinking grimly that her intuition had been right. Terrill Hawkes was about to return to his original form, wanting a conference immediately. 'I'll see him as soon as I shower and change,' she said, feeling suddenly underdressed for a conference in her casual clothes and still-braided hairdo.

Marisa shook her head. 'Mr Hawkes is at the pool.

He said to come there immediately.'

Claire sighed. Off and running, it seemed, with Marisa directing traffic. 'I'll go right there,' she said, giving Marisa a nod and a smile, and then passing through the *lanai* and looking down at the pool.

She expected to see Terrill Hawkes sitting at one of the poolside tables, fully dressed, a pile of papers before him, ready to pounce on her with a full slate of questions. Instead, there was only a large towel thrown over a poolside chair, and he was in the pool, swimming lazily back and forth with slow, powerful strokes. Claire found herself standing motionless, staring at him. She had seen him in his swimming trunks before at the pools in Las Vegas and Palm Springs, but had never seen him go into the water. She had always thought that perhaps he was not a swimmer. Now she could see that he definitely was, and an excellent one, his powerful legs and massive shoulders moving him through the water with effortless grace. It made a tight little knot form in her midsection, and she quickly looked away and descended the steps to the pool deck.

The scrape of the metal chair on the deck as she pulled it out to sit down alerted Terrill Hawkes to her presence. He swam to the edge, pulled himself out, and shook the water from his hair like a large spaniel.

'Hello, Claire,' he said, reaching for his towel and rubbing his head and face, then throwing the towel around his shoulders and giving her a warm smile. 'How are you?'

She stared at him, speechless. Terrill Hawkes had never called her Claire before in his life!

CHAPTER THREE

'ER—HELLO,' replied Claire uncertainly. 'I'm fine.'

This was not the usual form their meetings took. It was usually, 'Ah, there you are, Miss Forsythe. What have you to report?' The leopard's spots were definitely changing, but she had no idea what animal she was now seeing. She watched with a perplexed frown as he pushed himself to his feet with a little groan. His old football injury must be bothering him. That would account for his swimming. Swimming was supposed to be good for back problems. But it certainly was not enough to account for everything, especially what happened next.

Terrill Hawkes carefully spread his towel on the chair across the table from Claire and sat down, giving her a brief little smile as he did so.

'I think you could call me Terrill,' he said, glancing at her and then giving his attention to a speck on his forearm. 'I believe we've observed a proper period of formality.'

'Yes, I . . . er . . . I guess we have,' she replied, feeling as confused as if she'd suddenly discovered that green traffic lights now meant stop and red lights meant go.

'Well?' He glanced at her again, looked down, then seemed to force himself to look directly at her.

Well what? Claire wondered. Was it that he wanted her to say his name? Carry on a little chit-chatty conversation? She might as well try it as sit here with him staring at her like that, making her feel more uncomfortable by the minute.

'Well,' she drew the word out, 'hello, Terrill. How have you been? You look a little pale, compared to most of the tourists.' She blinked as he gave her a pleased smile. Apparently that had been what he wanted!

'I'm doing OK,' he replied, 'and I plan to become a more pleasing colour as quickly as possible. Both your tan and your hairstyle tell me you've been to Negril. They look good on you. I'm glad to see you're going native.'

'Thank you,' Claire said, feeling a little embarrassed at the unusual personal remark. 'Ernest took me to Negril yesterday. It's beautiful.'

Terrill nodded. 'Try the curried goat?' he asked.

'Yes. It was good. I liked it,' Claire replied. 'I didn't think I would, but I did.'

Terrill nodded again. 'I feel the same way about it. As long as I don't look at the baby goats, I'm all right. Did you get some honey bananas?'

'Oh, yes. Those are great. It's too bad they don't travel, isn't it?'

'Yes, it is. The papayas that reach the States are never as good as the ones here, either.'

'No, they certainly aren't.'

For what seemed to Claire like an eternity, this trivial conversation went on. It became obvious to her that Terrill was determined not to mention any business, and she became equally determined not to be the one to bring it up first. What was causing this strange behaviour, she had no idea. Except for looking a little tired, Terrill seemed perfectly normal. But she was sure that he was not when Marisa appeared on the balcony above them and announced that Terrill had a telephone call from a Mr Woodbine in New York. Payton Woodbine was vice president of Hawkes Hotels, famous for never disturbing his superior unless something important was afoot. This time, instead of leaping to his feet, Terrill made a face and sat perfectly still.

'Tell him I'm busy and I'll call him in the morning,' he said. He smiled at Claire, who was trying, unsuccessfully, not to look surprised. 'It'll keep,' he said. 'I think I'll take a nap until dinner. I had to get up awfully early this morning.'

'Good idea. You do look tired,' Claire agreed, getting to her feet at the same time as he did. She almost jumped out of her skin when he draped an arm around her shoulders and gave her a little squeeze.

'Everything here to your liking?' he asked.

'Oh, yes!' She glanced quickly up at him. 'It's just . . . just perfect.'

'Good.' He squeezed her shoulder again and then removed his arm. 'I'll see you at dinner, then,' he said, and strode off in the direction of the bedroom wing.

Claire sank down into one of the chairs on the balcony overlooking the pool, feeling dizzy. The mysteries about the hotel and Ben Williams paled beside the unaccountable change in the behaviour of the man she was now to call Terrill. Obviously he had decided to turn over some kind of new leaf. But why? What did it mean? She could just come right out and ask, but somehow she didn't think that was what Terrill wanted. In the past, he'd always expected her to figure things out for herself. That was her forte. But that was restricted to his wants in terms of the project she was working on. This was entirely different, and totally confusing. Her mind felt like one of those little glass balls filled with liquid, that you shook to turn a placid scene into a snowstorm, except that now the snow particles refused to settle again.

'There must be something I'm missing,' Claire muttered to a tiny lizard, who had climbed up to sun himself on the wrought-iron railing in front of her.

The lizard blinked and flicked its tongue out at her.

'Same to you,' Claire said, mimicking the little reptile. She got to her feet and headed for her room to put on her bathing-suit. Since it was futile to try and make sense of anything, she might as well take the rest of the day off herself and loll by the pool. Maybe by dinner time Terrill Hawkes would have recuperated enough to give her some clue about what was going on.

Her hopes were dashed as soon as she saw him approaching in response to Marisa's dinner bell. The man of many suits was wearing a wildly colourful silk robe, which stopped above his bare knees, and thong sandals on his bare feet. For all Claire could tell, he might be wearing nothing else at all! She tried to ignore that disturbing thought and keep her eyes focused above the large V of curly chest hair which the robe revealed.

'Thank you,' she said, looking somewhere past Terrill's left ear as he smiled a brief hello and held her chair for her. Thank goodness she had suspected something less than formal attire might be in order, and had put on a filmy print overblouse and white slacks and sandals. She would feel a perfect fool if she'd dressed for dinner.

'You look very nice,' he said, giving her another of those brief little smiles.

Funny, Claire thought. He seemed so reticent. Almost shy. It made her feel odd, as if she ought to encourage him or protect him. Lord knew, Terrill Hawkes didn't need encouraging or protecting!

'Thank you,' she said again. 'That's a spectacular robe. Did you get it in Jamaica?'

'Hong Kong,' Terrill replied, and they were off on a dinner conversation of the same calibre as their previous one.

Finally, as they sat by the railing at the edge of the pool deck and looked out over the circle of lights ringing Montego Bay, Claire could stand it no longer. What was going on? Why did Terrill keep giving her those funny little half-smiles without ever really looking her in the eye? If she didn't find out soon, she was going to explode. She licked her lips, then cleared her throat.

'Er . . . Terrill,' she said, still finding it difficult to call him by his first name, 'you seem . . . different. Is everything all right?'

'All right? Yes. Everything's fine. Why?'

'Well, I just thought . . .' Claire began, fumbling for some way to be tactful, '. . . I thought maybe you had something on your mind.'

Terrill frowned thoughtfully, and scratched the side of his neck. 'Actually, yes, I do have something on my mind,' he said finally, after which he stared out across the water for so long that Claire was hard pressed to keep from shouting, 'What?' 'It's not something I know quite how to bring up,' he said at last.

Claire groaned inwardly. At this rate, she would never find out, but she didn't want to pry into something that was none of her business.

'If you don't want to tell me . . .' she began.

'Oh, yes,' Terrill interrupted. 'I definitely do want to tell you.' He rubbed his chin, took a sip of his drink, then looked directly at Claire for the first time. 'Tell me, Claire,' he said, 'what do you think of the interior of the villa? I mean, the furnishings and all. Do you like them?'

The interior décor of the villa? That was what all of this strangeness was about? Claire cocked her head to one side and studied Terrill. No, he was leading up to something else, she decided. All she could do was play along and see where he went.

'Not very much,' she replied. 'I assumed they must be what you inherited from the previous owner.'

Terrill nodded. 'That's exactly what they are. Not very homey.'

'Sort of early airport lounge,' Claire agreed. 'Are you planning to have it redone?'

'Yes, it has to be.' He rubbed his neck again. 'I was hoping . . . that is . . . I'd like you to take charge of redoing it.'

'Me?' Claire cried, leaning forward and staring at him incredulously. 'Besides doing the hotel?' The man had lost his mind! He must thing she had forty-eight hours in her days, not twenty-four.

'Don't worry about the hotel,' Terrill said quickly. 'It won't go away.'

'No, but it won't go anywhere, either. Besides, I'm not a decorator.'

'That's just the point. I plan to spend a good deal of time here in the future. I want something comfortable and homey, not some slick professional job. You know what I like by now, I should think.'

Claire felt her irritation growing. It was time to get some answers. 'I don't understand what's going on. First you give me that "time is of the essence" line to get me down here. Now, you say that the hotel can wait while I work on your villa. Has all of this got something to do with that strange question you asked me back in New York? The one about whether you were too old to reform or not?'

Terrill gave her another quick, and this time very penetrating, look. Then he smiled, a sort of mysterious, inward-directed smile, and looked down. 'It has everything to do with that,' he replied very quietly.

That wasn't much of an answer, Claire thought wryly, but it was a start. 'Then,' she went on, 'am I to assume that your desire to spend more time here in a homey atmosphere means you've decided to conduct your—er—love-life at a slower pace? And you're going to pick ladies who don't go so much for the glitter and glamour routine, but like a more quiet ambience?'

'You're partly right.' The mysterious little smile continued. 'Actually, I don't intend to pick any ladies at all of the type of which you're probably referring, at least for the foreseeable future. And I intend to conduct my entire life at a slower pace.'

'Oh.' Claire leaned back in her chair again, disconcerted by his answer. Now, she thought, they were getting closer to the heart of the matter. Perhaps that smile was not so much mysterious as a cover for the fact that Terrill was ill at ease revealing such a change, afraid she would demand too many answers that he was not ready to give. For, surely, something drastic must have happened to make him consider such changes. 'Well,' she said to reassure him, 'I must say that I thoroughly approve. And yes, I'll be happy to see what I can do with the villa. You don't mind if I see if Ernest has a relative who specialises in decorating, do you? I may need some help, and his family seems to be into just about every profession.'

A subtle change around the eyes told Claire that Terrill was now very pleased.

'No, I don't mind at all. Thank you, Claire.' He looked off across the harbour again. 'I suppose you're wondering why,' he said, as if he had read Claire's earlier thoughts.

'Yes,' she said, 'but if you'd rather not discuss it now . . .'

'I said I wanted to, didn't I?' he replied, a trace of his old irritation reappearing. Then he smiled almost sheepishly. 'I'm sorry. I appreciate your tact, as always. You see, I've been doing some thinking lately about my life. Alternating between working too hard and playing too hard doesn't seem to add up to what I thought life was all about. It was fun for a while, but it's not enough. I don't want to wake up some morning and find that my life is over and I've missed . . . so many things. Sunsets, and quiet walks, and . . .' He stopped, a catch in his voice. A look of deep sadness flitted briefly across his face, quickly masked by one of those little smiles.

'Time to smell the roses?' Claire finished for him softly. This was a side of Terrill Hawkes that she had never seen before, had never suspected existed. She had seen his sensitivity to the cares of others, of course, but she hadn't known that he brooded about the meaning of his own life. He must have done so for quite a while to have finally reached this stage of decision.

'That's the gist of it,' he agreed. 'I've felt I was not only running myself ragged, but you, too. I thought that if I could get you to Jamaica, then we could both slow down. I hope you don't find that idea too unpleasant.'

'Unpleasant? No, of course not,' Claire replied quickly. 'I've thought for some time that if you didn't slow down, you'd burn yourself out before you were forty. And I've already found it very easy to take things more slowly here. It would seem almost sinful to put on blinkers and go rushing past all the beautiful sights.'

'I'm so glad you feel that way,' Terrill said, looking relieved. 'What do you say to taking the rest of this week off entirely? No mention of business at all. I can take you around to see a lot of the famous tourist sights, and some others that the tourists seldom see. I haven't been here in a long time, except for buying the hotel, of course, and I'd like to see it all again.'

'That sounds wonderful,' Claire agreed, although Terrill's mention of being here to buy the hotel jogged a sharp little corner in her memory. She wanted to ask him why he had never mentioned it before, but decided to wait until their week of vacation from all business was up. Perhaps she'd find out something during that week, anyway.

CHAPTER FOUR

CLAIRE felt her nerves jingling with anticipation the next morning. Memories of her early attempt to get closer to Terrill Hawkes kept trying to intrude into her thoughts, along with all too vivid memories of his rejection of her. She had thought that one kiss was forgotten, but found that it had sprung to life overnight, a phantom that had been banished by her strong will, but was only waiting to discover a tiny breach in her armour to haunt her again.

'For goodness' sake, don't act the love-starved career woman,' she scolded herself while she dressed in the casual clothes that Terrill had prescribed before they parted the night before. Terrill was only trying to get his own life in order. He had given no sign of any interest in her, other than as a friend, and probably wouldn't. It was quite apparent from what he had said that one of the things he had decided was out of hand was his relationship with women. Besides, she knew him far too well now to ever fall victim to the kind of starry-eyed crush she had had on him at first.

Nevertheless, Claire felt her heartbeat quicken when Terrill arose from the table, where he had been reading the newspaper and drinking an early cup of coffee, and greeted her with a warm smile.

'Good morning, Claire. You're looking fresh as a sea breeze.'

'Good morning, Terrill,' she replied, still feeling

66

strange about calling him by his first name. There was no way that she could tell him that he looked like every woman's dream of the kind of man she would like to have greet her across the breakfast table. Not that he hadn't doubtless been told that many times before, she reminded herself. 'Have you decided where we're going today?' she asked, sitting down quickly and concentrating her attention on the grapefruit half, sprinkled with coarse Jamaican sugar, that Marisa put before her.

'Marisa needs to do some shopping,' Terrill replied, 'so I thought we'd take her. The market is very different from your neighbourhood super-markets in the States. I thought you'd like to see it. Then, this afternoon, we can visit the bird sanctuary at Anchovy. Maybe you'll get to feed the doctor birds.'

'Doctor bird?' Claire asked. 'What kind of bird is that?'

'The native Jamaican humming-bird. It has a divided tail this long.' Terrill held up his hands to illustrate. 'I didn't believe it the first time I saw one. They're used to visitors, and come right up to be fed at the sanctuary.'

'What fun! My mother's quite a bird-watcher,' Claire said. 'We used to put up a lot of feeders for the birds in the winter, but, of course, the birds weren't tame at all, and we had to be careful where we put the feeders so that barn cats couldn't get to them.'

'Barn cats? I didn't know you grew up on a farm,' Terrill said. 'I spent part of my youth on a ranch in Texas.' He frowned and shook his head. 'How could I have not known? Did you never mention it, or wasn't I listening?'

'We never discussed anything except business,' Claire replied, feeling uncomfortable under the intense scrutiny Terrill was now giving her. 'I did know you grew up on a ranch, though. I've seen it mentioned in articles about you.'

Terrill sighed. 'That certainly proves what I was saying last night, doesn't it? As closely as we've worked together, and we're still almost strangers.'

You could say that again, Claire thought. Terrill looked quite distressed, his sparkling blue eyes cloudy. Only a short time ago she couldn't have imagined him caring whether she had a childhood on a farm or popped full-grown out of a catalogue, ready to work for him. She smiled at him encouragingly.

'The story of my life isn't that long and complicated,' she said. 'It won't take you long to get caught up on the details.'

'At least if I hear it from you it will be true,' Terrill said. 'That story about the Texas ranch is only half-true. My parents separated when I was twelve, and my mother and I moved to town. Otherwise, I'd probably not have played football. My father wouldn't let my older brothers waste their time like that.'

'Sounds like a stern sort of man,' Claire commented. 'I guess a lot of farmers are. My father was pretty strict about doing chores first, too. Then he decided to go back to college himself and study animal genetics, and we all moved to town. I was about twelve then myself. We still had a big yard, though, and a funny old dilapidated sort of barn in the back. And cats.'

'I don't like cats very much,' Terrill said. 'I love dogs, though. Do you like dogs?'

'I love them,' Claire replied. 'Actually, I love cats, too. And cows and horses.'

Terrill nodded. 'An animal lover. I thought you would be. Maybe we should get a dog. There's plenty of room here. Marisa?' He addressed the housekeeper, who was replenishing their plate of scrambled eggs and bacon. 'Would you mind if I got a dog?'

'No, sir,' she replied. 'I like dogs. Especially a good watchdog, if it isn't mean.'

'I'll look for one,' he said, smiling as happily as a young boy at the prospect. 'I haven't had a dog since I was a boy.'

Something inside Claire melted at the sight of that smile. She had seen Terrill Hawkes smile in triumph before, she had seen the seductive smile he gave to his current love-interest, she had seen the warm, friendly smile with which he greeted friends. But the smile she saw now was the first truly happy smile she had ever seen, a smile as sunny and delighted as a child's. It was a smile she would like to see much more often, she thought as she watched his face. She realised she had been staring when Terrill suddenly cocked his head, one eyebrow raised questioningly.

'A penny for your thoughts,' he said.

'Oh . . .' Claire blushed. 'I was just trying to imagine . . .' She stopped again. What she had really been trying to imagine was what it would be like to have him be that happy at seeing her, a ridiculous idea to even contemplate. 'I was trying to picture,' she said firmly, regaining her composure, 'the perfect dog for you. I think it would have to be rather large. Maybe a German shepherd or a golden retriever.'

'A golden retriever sounds nice,' Terrill said

thoughtfully. 'They're usually good-tempered, too, aren't they?'

'All the ones I've known are,' Claire replied.

They continued discussing the merits of different breeds of dogs over breakfast, injecting little details of their lives as they went along. When the table was cleared, Ernest brought the van around and Terrill drove them to the central market in Montego Bay.

'This is fascinating!' Claire exclaimed, watching as Marisa went from one display stand to another in the huge, open-sided building, picking the finest fruit from one, a pile of fresh vegetables from another. At each display was the producer of the goods, eager to show off the virtues of his or her wares. Tucked in a cosy niche between some corn and squash at one stand was a peacefully sleeping infant, but in most there were only melons and papaya, pineapple and plantain and oranges, jars of red beans, peppers and green beans and tomatoes and pumpkins.

'I make pumpkin soup,' Marisa said, when Claire asked how she planned to use the one she had picked. 'You will see, tonight,' she added with a mischievous twinkle, when Claire's eyes widened at that announcement.

Claire smiled up at Terrill, who was standing beside her, watching very soberly. 'This is much more fun than the supermarket,' she said. 'Even if it took longer, I'd much rather shop this way.' She was rewarded with a smile so dazzling that it almost took her breath away.

'I seem to have guessed right again,' he said softly. His arm stole around Claire and his hand rested lightly on her waist.

'Guessed right?' she said, trying to think what on

earth he might be talking about with a mind that
suddenly seemed to want to think of nothing but that
hand and arm that were touching her more firmly
now.

'That you'd enjoy the market,' he replied. 'I like
it better, too. No middle man. No plastic wraps.
Everything fresh from the garden.'

'Oh, yes,' Claire agreed, slipping free of his grasp
before it could disturb her equilibrium further.
'Look, there are some baskets and hats.' She moved
to another stand, picking up a fat, long-handled
basket and admiring it, while in a corner of her mind
questions about what Terrill Hawkes might be up to
were beginning to niggle uncomfortably. Never, in
the three years since they had met, had she known
him to do anything without some clear purpose in
mind. She had better keep her feet firmly on the
ground, lest the undeniable attraction she still felt
for him in his newly benevolent state lead her astray.

'That would be good for holding magazines,'
Terrill said, moving to her side again. 'Shall we buy
it?'

'Yes, let's,' Claire said, enchanted at the happy
smile that came to the face of the pretty Jamaican
girl who was the maker of the basket. There was,
indeed, something especially nice about meeting the
producer of the goods you bought, face to face.

They followed Marisa to the fish market across the
way, where she eyed the catch critically and rejected
several fat blue fish before finding one she liked.
Then they got back into the van and travelled
through several streets to a baker's shop, and after
that stopped at a meat market in a small shopping
centre, where Claire bought a necklace from a
woman peddling her handmade wares under an

umbrella on the pavement.

'Still think you'd prefer Jamaican shopping?' Terrill asked, when they arrived back at the villa after noon.

'Not every day,' Claire admitted, 'but I could stand it once or twice a week.'

They took a leisurely swim in the pool, and had a light lunch before starting for the bird sanctuary. Terrill did not repeat his attempt to touch Claire, but she felt his eyes upon her frequently, and when she looked at him he smiled. It was not quite the seductive smile she had seen him use on other women, but there was something deeply warm and disturbing in his eyes. At least, she felt that there was. Or was it only her imagination, spurred by her own quickening pulse? She tried to look at it objectively, but found that she could not, finally deciding to give up and enjoy it while it lasted. She was still not convinced that Terrill Hawkes could have changed so completely in such record time.

But Terrill was the perfect gentleman at the bird sanctuary, his entrancement with the tiny doctor birds so genuine that Claire could easily have believed that he spent all of his time enjoying nature, rather than piling up his fortune. When one of the birds came to drink from the vial of sweetened water that he held, he scarcely breathed.

'Wasn't that marvellous?' he whispered, that wide, boyish smile again lighting his face.

'Better than that,' Claire whispered back, controlling an almost irresistible urge to throw her arms around him and tell him to stay that way for ever.

That smile did not come often during the rest of the week, although Terrill did seem happy enough, taking great pleasure in showing Claire the tourist sights along the north coast from Montego Bay to Ocho Rios. He put his arm around her now and then, but smiled and seemed not to mind when she pulled away, still suspicious of his motives. When they speculated over the witch's ghost said to inhabit the Rose Hall mansion, she was tempted to ask about the ghost on the beach, but decided against it, fearing it would only break their pleasant mood. They rode the Governor's Coach train into the mountains, rafted on the Martha Brae river, saw the sight of Columbus' early landing at Discovery Bay. But when Claire stood at the foot of the six-hundred-foot height of Dunn's River Falls and announced, with shaking knees, that she was scared to death to attempt the climb, he again put a gentle arm around her.

'Why don't you take the stairs?' he suggested. 'I'll go up with the guide and tell you all about it. Or you could ask that nice little grey-haired lady who's about half-way up now.'

Claire looked up and caught the gleam of mischief lighting his blue eyes.

'Are you suggesting that I'm chicken?' she asked.

'Why, Claire, would I do that?' he asked in return, and then burst into hearty laughter, his gentle touch turning into a hug that left Claire gasping for breath and feeling that she had no alternative but to grin and bear the experience.

'Well, how was it?' he asked when they at last reached the top.

'Claire shook her head, looking back at the cascading water. 'That was,' she said soberly, 'the most fantastic, exciting thing I've ever done.' She smiled up at her tall companion. 'I loved it.' Her knees began to quiver again when she was rewarded with one of those sunny smiles and another huge hug.

By Saturday night, Claire was ready to admit to herself that she had been wrong about Terrill Hawkes. The one she had seen all week must be the real man; the driven, sometimes violent-tempered man she had known, a disguise for the gentle man beneath. She still had no clue for the reason for the change, other than the one he had given, but she no longer cared. She wanted to keep him this way, and if he were to take her in his arms again she wouldn't run away and break the wonderful spell the week together had cast over them.

After several nights of dining out, Marisa was to treat them with a feast of Jamaican lobster that night, and Terrill had suggested that they dress for dinner in order to pay her adequate tribute for her efforts. Claire dressed with special care in a long dress of soft, peach-coloured gauze. It had a modest, square neckline and short, puffy sleeves. Not, she thought with an unpleasant chill of memory, the sort Terrill would call an obvious come-on. He might even consider it a bit too much the *ingénue* for her.

But he apparently did not. When he saw her and smiled that special smile only for her, Claire felt her heart almost stand still. Terrill Hawkes had never looked more handsome, the immaculate white of his dinner-jacket accenting the breadth of his shoulders and the dark tan he had already acquired.

'You look like an angel,' he said softly, taking her arm and escorting her gallantly to her chair.

'Thank you, sir,' she replied, feeling her cheeks grow warm with pleasure and happiness. 'You look pretty special yourself.'

There was such an electricity in the air that Claire scarcely knew what she was eating. Something was going to happen tonight. A tangible force seemed to constantly be drawing their eyes to meet. Now and then a thought flitted through Claire's mind that perhaps she ought to still be a little wary, but she buried such thoughts with light-hearted laughter and the bubbles from several glasses of champagne. Nothing was going to spoil this marvellous evening.

'Shall we dance?' Terrill asked, taking Claire's hand when dinner was over.

'I thought you didn't dance,' she replied, reminded once again of that painful experience so long ago.

Terrill squeezed her hand, as if in understanding. 'I don't, really,' he said, 'but if it's slow enough I can fake it. Shall we put some records on the stereo?'

'All right,' Claire agreed. 'I'd like that.' More than dancing, she was, she knew, hungry for the feeling of Terrill's arms around her. It might be foolish, it might be crazy, but she could not deny it any longer.

The rug had already been removed from the tiled floor of the large living-room, the furniture pushed back, evidence that Terrill had planned for dancing. He confirmed it as soon as he took Claire into his arms.

'I thought that if we danced I might be able to touch you without you slipping away,' he said softly into Claire's ear.

'Good thinking,' she replied, smiling up at him as he pulled her tightly against him. She felt as if every bubble in the champagne she had drunk was still floating inside of her, making her light and airy as the breeze that wafted through the wide-flung louvred doors. When Terrill lowered his cheek to press against hers, she thought she might soon be

flying. She closed her eyes, revelling in the warmth
of his strong arms around her and the solid male
firmness of his body.

'Shall we take a break outside?' Terrill asked after
the record had finished.

Claire nodded, a little regretfully, for she knew
she could easily have danced all night. She did
remember, though, that Terrill's back might bother
him if they kept dancing too long. He kept an arm
around her as they walked to the railing of the pool
deck. An almost full moon was leaving a trail of
diamonds across the water of the bay below.

'Beautiful, isn't it?' Claire murmured.

'Yes,' Terrill replied. 'More beautiful than I
remembered.'

There was a husky quality to Terrill's voice that
made Claire look up at him quickly.

'What's wrong, Terrill?' she asked, catching a
glimpse of an almost haunted look that he quickly
masked with a smile.

'Nothing,' he replied. Then he smiled more
broadly as she frowned at him. 'You do know me
rather well, don't you?' he said. 'I guess I might as
well confess that I was thinking that it's really too
bad we've wasted so much time. I've thought for
some time that if we could ever get out of that
pattern of screaming at each other that we would be
able to establish a much better relationship.'

'Better . . . relationship?' Claire said, her own
voice almost failing her. What did he mean by that?
She searched his face, feeling her whole body begin
to tremble at the intensity of his gaze.

Terrill nodded. He turned Claire to face him and
put both arms around her. 'You, Miss Claire
Forsythe,' he said very seriously, 'are the most

interesting, exciting woman I've ever met.' He lowered his head. 'And by far the most beautiful,' he added, just before his mouth found Claire's.

For a few seconds, Claire stood like a statue, trying to take in the import of Terrill's words, words she had never even dreamed she might hear from him on this night. Then the message from those soft lips took over and everything else vanished. She felt as if the world, and her heart, had stopped completely. A shower of warmth rushed over her and through her, setting her afire with excitement. This was the way she had always imagined it would be to kiss that wide, sensuous mouth and be held next to that big, muscular body, in those dreamy days before he had punished her with a kiss designed to destroy those dreams. Now, her mind registered dimly that it was every bit as wonderful as she had imgained. Her arms circled his broad back, helping to hold her upright in a reeling universe, while her mouth opened to permit the invasion of an alien she felt she had always known. Even the formal dress that they both wore this evening was little barrier to the knowledge of their mutual arousal, and that knowledge made Claire moan softly, deep in her throat, and press more tightly against him. Terrill responded with a low groan, his hands moulding her to him, his body moving sensuously against hers.

Oh, lord, how I want him! Claire thought, desire aching through her. All of these years she had repressed that thought, but now it was rocketing to the foreground, like a wild, unleashed animal.

'Oh, Claire, I want you so much.' Terrill's voice was deep with passion. 'We could have such wonderful times together.'

Wonderful times? Claire opened her eyes. Her

mind began to function again. Terrill's eyes were so close, so dark, the centres wide and black with desire. He wanted her, oh, yes, he wanted her. And she wanted him. There was no denying that. But how many other women had stood exactly where she stood, wanting and being wanted, by a man who swore he would never marry? Did she want him enough to give up everything she believed in and become what she knew he now wanted her for—his mistress? For a short period of 'wonderful times'?

She felt the beginning of a sob catch in her throat. What a fool she had been! He had it all planned so cleverly, this past unbelievably warm and gentle week with him. He would wean her away from her job, so that she wouldn't even mind leaving it to spend all of her time in her bed or on his arm. And he would keep her here, at his villa in Jamaica, made quiet and homey. She wasn't glamorous enough for the spots he took his other women! With a strangled sound, she thrust him from her.

'Stop it! Stop it! Stop it!' she cried, twisting herself free and pushing him away as he tried to pull her back. 'Don't touch me!' She backed away, gasping for breath, and trying to make her head stop spinning from the sickening revelation. 'Don't talk to me any more,' she grated, shaking her head as Terrill opened his mouth as if to speak. 'I should have known all along. Oh, I suspected. No one changes overnight as much as you claimed to have done. But you were so clever, I almost believed you. I wanted to believe you. I guess after three years you had me figured out pretty well. But there's one thing you forgot. I don't want to be your mistress, or anyone else's, for that matter. I don't know what's wrong with you, that you have to try to possess every woman who temporarily catches your fancy, but it's not something I can cope with. I don't even want to try. I'm going to my room now, and in the morning I'm going to pack up and get out of here. I don't think we can work together any more. Goodbye, Terrill Hawkes. I quit! And this time I really mean it!'

With that, she turned and fled towards her room, ignoring the sound of Terrill calling after her, 'Claire, wait! Please!' and then wincing at the sound of glass crashing and shattering against the concrete deck below.

CHAPTER FIVE

CLAIRE scurried into her room, tears streaming down her cheeks, and slammed the door behind her. As an afterthought, she turned and locked the door. If she knew the real Terrill Hawkes, he'd be pounding on the door in a few minutes, roaring out his displeasure. He was.

'Claire, let me in!' he shouted, after a few bangs on the door that left the entire wall shuddering. 'You're over-reacting. I have no intention of forcing you into doing anything you don't want to do. For God's sake, at least think about what you're doing, will you?'

'I am,' she yelled back between gulped sobs. 'I think I'm the biggest fool in the world to have fallen for your line. I'm packing right now, so don't stand out there yelling at me. Go away!' She grabbed her large suitcase from the bottom of her wardrobe, threw it on her bed and opened it, then began piling her clothes into it helter-skelter.

'What in the devil are you so afraid of?' came the next roar. 'Is there some reason you can't enjoy being a woman and doing your job, too? I didn't intend for you to quit.'

'That's not what you said the last time,' Claire hollered back, yanking down the zipper on her dress and stepping out of it. She shivered, then found her robe and slipped it on. 'I have no desire to get into an affair with no future,' she added. 'Last I heard, you didn't believe in love and marriage. Or are you going

80

to try and tell me now that that's all changed?'

'No, I'm not going to try and tell you anything! When you get everything set in your mind, a person might as well talk to a wall! Go ahead and quit. I'm damned if I'll even give you a decent recommendation. Who would want to put up with anyone as pigheaded as you are?'

'That's exactly what I've wondered about you!' Claire shouted to the beat of Terrill's retreating footsteps.

At the sound of his door crashing shut, Claire sank down on her bed and beat her fist into the pile of clothing in frustration. Why, oh, why had she let herself be taken in by Terrill Hawkes' act? Maybe because it had been so very convincing. He had been so sweet, so lovable, so believable. Slowing down, was he? Shifting into a higher gear was more like it! Well, at least she had the grim satisfaction of knowing that he'd had to put on quite a show in order to almost trap her.

Actually, she admitted to herself with a weary sigh as she trudged into her bathroom and splashed cold water on her tear-stained face, it hadn't been all that hard for him to do. There wasn't any other man she'd ever met who could turn her on as Terrill Hawkes could. It was just as well if she did get away from him now. Otherwise, she'd probably never be able to get interested in anyone else, and she really did want to marry and have a family some day. If only Terrill . . .

'Forget it!' she snapped, scowling at her own reflection. He wasn't in love with her, and she certainly wasn't in love with him. It was only a physical attraction. A very strong physical attraction. She walked back to her bedside and began folding the pile of clothing more carefully. Yes, it was time to really

quit, once and for all. She liked and respected a lot of
things about Terrill Hawkes, but she didn't respect his
attitude towards women. Even if a woman could trap
him into marriage, she'd never be able to trust him.

Her suitcases finally packed, Claire lay down on her
bed. She did not feel like sleeping. A deep, miserable
ache had settled into her midsection. She got up again
and wandered back to her bathroom, feeling around in
her medicine cabinet for a bottle of antacid pills.

'I suppose I could pack this stuff,' she muttered,
finally switching on the light. She shook her head.
Might as well leave her make-up and other toiletries
until morning. But would she be able to get an early
flight? She would just as soon not have to stay around
and get into another shouting match with Terrill. In
fact, she would as soon not see him at all. A shaky,
weak feeling that would not bear close scrutiny was
beginning to replace her earlier bravado. It would be a
good idea to get her plane reservation right now, if she
could, before she had second thoughts.

There were only two phones in the villa, one in the
kitchen and one in the office. There was no privacy in
the kitchen, where Marisa often pottered about until
quite late, so Claire tiptoed quietly to the office and
listened at the door. She had heard Terrill in there at
night a couple of times, pecking slowly at the
typewriter, but all was quiet now. She let herself in,
closed the door behind her, and groped her way
through the darkness to the desk, where she fumbled
for the switch on the lamp and turned it on. Terrill had
indeed been there, she observed wryly, for the waste-
paper basket was full of crumpled papers. She sat
down at the desk and picked up the telephone
directory. A business card fell from between the pages
and landed in her lap. She picked it up and looked at it

curiously. It was a doctor's card. The address and telephone numbers were of the Mayo Clinic, Rochester, Minnesota.

A chill went through Claire's body so quickly that her hands and feet turned instantly cold and clammy. her head felt light and dizzy. The Mayo Clinic? That was where Terrill had gone? What was wrong with him? Was he seriously ill?

Don't be silly, she told herself, half annoyed at her shaking hand that held the card. It's probably just his old football injury acting up. Some of the world's finest specialists were at Mayo's. He'd probably just gone for a check-up, and to see if anything could be done for his back. It couldn't be much fun, living with that constant pain. He often winced, ever so slightly, when he had to bend, or when he got up after sitting for a long time.

But, said a chilling little voice inside her, what if they had discovered something much worse? What if Terrill had suddenly been forced to face the fact that his very life might be in jeopardy? That could well explain why he had said, 'I don't want to wake up some morning and find that my life is over and I've missed . . . so many things.'

Claire could hear the deepness of Terrill's voice, see Terrill's face before her as if he were in the room, the quickly concealed look of desolate sadness stopping for her now like a frozen frame of a movie. Good lord, he hadn't been trying to deceive her! It was real! And, like the fool she was, she had missed or misinterpreted all of the signs: that strange telephone call, no doubt because he needed to hear a familiar voice; his wanting the villa to be quiet and homey; even his wanting her to assume a new role now, someone who didn't demand wild parties and extravagant entertainments.

The slight trembling that Claire had felt became so violent that she jumped to her feet and grasped the edge of the desk, fighting for enough stability to return to her room.

'Dear God,' she whispered. 'Dear, dear God. Please tell me it isn't . . . something awful!' Terrill Hawkes might be the most aggravating, annoying, deceptive man in the world, but a world without Terrill Hawkes . . . was unthinkable!

Her mind numb with anguish, Claire tucked the card back into the telephone directory, turned out the light, and staggered from the room, waves of nausea sweeping over her. Attempts to tell herself to get hold of herself did no good. Feeling as if she might become physically sick at any moment, she rushed into her bathroom and leaned over the basin, weak and shaking, tears streaming down her face.

'Dear lord, I love him so much,' she sobbed. 'I was so stupid not to see it. Please don't take him away from me now.'

Then she did become miserably sick, feeling as if her heart were being torn out along with everything she had eaten in years. Afterwards she flushed and mopped the horrid remains away, then splashed and splashed her face with cold water, trying desperately to regain some control and be able to think. All her mind would produce were images of Terrill, each one more dear than the last.

A loud pounding sounded on her door.

'What in the devil are you doing in there?' came a typical Terrill Hawkes roar. 'I can't get any cold water.'

'N-nothing,' Claire replied. 'I was just getting cleaned up.' Her hand shook so as she reached into her bath cabinet for some mouthwash that she knocked half a dozen bottles over, and they fell to the basin below with a clatter. Almost immediately, she heard her door open.

'Claire? What's going on in there? Are you all right?' The roar was reduced to a husky growl.

Terrill was coming! Oh, lord, she had to get herself together. She began shoving the bottles back into the cabinet.

'I'm fine!' she called out hoarsely. 'I just mouthed my dropwash! I mean, I was going to wash my bottles . . . Oh, damn!' A hastily replaced bottle had teetered and then precipitated another cascade of bottles back to the basin below.

The bedroom door was flung open and the light came on. Muffled footsteps crossed the floor.

'Claire, what on earth . . .'

'Don't come in!' Claire grabbed hastily for a towel to cover her thin nightgown, then lunged for the bathroom door, but it was too late. Terrill was standing there, dressed only in a large towel wrapped around his waist, sarong fashion. She stared at him, the room swaying crazily around her.

'I was taking a shower and suddenly there was no cold water. You damn near scalded me,' Terrill began, his displeasure obvious. He scowled, then raised his eyebrows. 'Claire, what is it? What's the matter?' He flung his arms out and caught her as she lurched forward and clung to him. 'Good lord, what a mess,' he said, suddenly able to see past her into the bathroom.

'Oh, Terrill,' she squeaked, clutching him, her sobs beginning anew. 'I'm so s-sorry.'

'Are you sick?' he asked, concern replacing the gruffness in his voice.

Claire nodded, her cheek rubbing against the roughness of Terrill's chest. She wanted to hold him like this for ever, and never let anything hurt him.

'Poor baby.' His voice was suddenly soft. A gentle hand smoothed her hair and then rested on her forehead. 'You don't feel feverish. Was it something you ate, do you think?'

'I . . . I guess so,' she choked out. There wasn't anything else she could tell him. He'd think she was crazy if she suddenly blurted out that she loved him, and he obviously didn't want anyone to know he was ill.

'Do you want to go back to bed now?'

Oh, lord, did she! She wanted him there beside her, so that she could hold him and comfort him and love him. But that wasn't what he wanted, and she mustn't let him know she'd guessed. With a painful effort she loosened her grip and looked up at his worried face. She couldn't bear to have him worried because of her. He had enough to worry about already.

'I'm all right now,' she said, with a pitiful attempt at a smile. 'I'll just pick up my mess and then go to bed. I won't run any more cold water and spoil your shower. I'm very sorry about that.'

'Oh, Claire.' Terrill shook his head. 'Always so brave and independent. You're the colour of a ghost. Come on, back to bed. The maid can clean up for you in the morning.' He lifted Claire as if she were a feather and carried her to her bed, tucking the covers around her and then laying his hand along her cheek again. 'You're to stay in bed in the morning,' he said, trying to sound severe, but betraying his concern by the anxious lines around his eyes. 'If you're not feeling a hundred per cent better by noon, we'll get a doctor to look at you. And I'm afraid I'm going to have to insist that you put off leaving for a day or two.'

'B—but . . . all right,' Claire said, a new wave of despair sweeping over her. Only a day or two? Now Terrill didn't even want her to stay on. Tears trickled from the corners of her eyes.

'What's wrong, Claire?' Terrill asked, bending to peer into her eyes. 'Are you that anxious to go?'

'Oh, no,' Claire replied quickly. 'There's no hurry.' She'd do anything now, if he'd only let her stay. Anything at all!

Terrill looked at the row of suitcases by the foot of Claire's bed and then back at her, one eyebrow cocked upward.

'I'll tell the maid to unpack your things,' he said. 'They get wrinkled very quickly in this humidity.' He hitched the towel more tightly around him and then walked to the door, pausing with his hand on the light-switch. 'By the way, Claire,' he said, 'I haven't been lying to you. Not once.' With that, he turned off the light and went quietly out of the door.

Claire turned her face into the pillow, sobbing silently. She knew that now. Why had she never realised before that he was the most wonderful man in the world? She must be the stupidest woman who ever lived! Utterly miserable, she fell into a deep, troubled sleep.

It was still quite early when she awoke, feeling almost normal except for terrible hunger pangs and a deep longing to see Terrill again. She wanted to look at him, to see if she could see any sign of what might be wrong. That thought made the ache start in Claire's heart again, and she shut her eyes. She had to learn not to think about that, she thought grimly, unless there was something she could do. What could she do? She could see that he wasn't suddenly left with the hotel renovation in his hands. In order to do that, she would have to stay on for more than a few days. And, if he still wanted her . . .

Claire sat up, pushing her hair back from her face with an impatient hand. She was definitely going to stay. He needed her more than ever before. And, if he really wanted her, she was his for the asking. But first things first. She'd have to give some indication that she'd changed her mind about quitting, without appearing too eager to stay. There was no way he could know she'd seen that telltale card, but he was so astute, and he knew her so well, that if she were to suddenly appear too agreeable, he might become suspicious. She'd have to appear at least a little reluctant, a little argumentative. Something, she thought wryly, she'd had plenty of practice at doing.

A gnawing feeling in Claire's stomach reminded her of the sorry events of the night before. No wonder she was starving now!

'Maybe I could sneak at least a glass of juice and some fruit,' she muttered. Then she could climb back into bed and pretend she'd been following Terrill's orders. He never took kindly to someone disobeying a direct order, and there was no point in starting a fight over that. She slipped from her bed, donned her robe and slippers, then padded quietly down the hall and the long balcony to the kitchen. She had just poured herself a glass of orange juice from the pitcher in the refrigerator, when she heard Marisa's voice, calling to one of the housemaids as she came closer.

With her glass of juice in one hand, Claire scurried back towards her room, giving only a wistful glance at the bowl of fruit on the dining-table. As she passed Terrill's door she heard him sneeze and then blow his nose. She was just reaching for her doorknob when she heard his door opening behind her.

Putting on a burst of speed, Claire bolted across her room, caught her toe on the abominable little throw rug, and crashed headlong on to her bed, cracking her shin smartly against the hard bedframe.

'Oh! Darn it!' Claire cried as juice flew in all directions, a large portion of it landing on her face. She heard Terrill's footsteps, clopping along in rubber beach sandals, dashing towards her room.

'Claire, what are you doing up?'

Drat! He had seen her and he sounded cross. The footsteps paused at her door.

'Claire, what in the devil happened now? Are you all right?'

'I'm just fine,' she muttered grimly, wiping orange juice from her face with a corner of the bedsheet. 'And don't you dare yell at me! I only wanted a glass of juice. It's not my fault that stupid rug tripped me and this stupid bed almost broke my leg!' She gathered her shattered dignity and turned to sit on the edge of the bed. Terrill was aproaching her now, wearing a white terry beach robe and a dark-browed frown. Obviously, he had been interrupted on his way to an early morning swim.

He shook his head, sighed, and then sat down beside her, his frown changing to a grudging little smile.

'You've turned into a regular Calamity Jane,' he said drily. 'At least I assume you're feeling better this morning. You're looking pink and healthy enough again.'

'I said I was fine,' she replied, thinking how cruelly deceiving it was that Terrill also looked so vitally strong and healthy. Having him so near in such intimate surroundings was already working devilish tricks on her equilibrium, and she looked down, studying her sticky fingers intently. 'I'm hungry,' she said, trying to sound cross. 'Can I get up now?'

'Maybe. On one condition.'

'What's that?' Claire asked, flicking a glance up at him and affecting a sulky expression.

'That you agree to stay on and work on the Jamaican Star. I would find it very . . . inconvenient to have to find someone else right now.'

The sound of those words and the gruff huskiness of Terrill's voice made Claire's heart begin to ache almost unbearably. She had never dreamed he might actually ask her to stay on. That was as close as he could come to admitting that he needed her, additional confirmation that he was not well enough to do the job alone or with a novice assistant. But, rather than blurt out that she certainly would stay, she set her jaw and gave him a belligerent frown.

'What if I won't?' she asked.

Terrill frowned back. 'Then, damn it, I'll lock you in this room until you agree to stay. And in between I may ravish you a few times for good measure. It's time you learned to act like a woman, instead of a female version of a hooked fish, trying to spit out the bait. In fact,' he added, smiling grimly as Claire's eyes widened, 'I'd do it right now if you weren't so sticky.' He suddenly bent towards Claire and kissed her lips firmly, just as quickly drawing back. 'There. Didn't hurt much, did it?'

Claire only stared at him reprovingly, trying to stifle an insane desire to giggle at the idea that she minded at all, and an equally wild wish that she weren't too sticky to be ravished at the moment. When the silence continued for several minutes, Terrill finally spoke.

'Well, does your unusual lack of a reply mean you'll

stay, or shall I have your breakfast sent in to you?'

'Oh, all right, I'll stay,' Claire replied, hoping she sounded grudging, while all the time she wondered if Terrill would ever know that he would have had to carry her kicking and screaming to the airport if he wanted her to go.

Terrill caught Claire's chin between his thumb and forefinger, and looked at her intently.

'Does your reluctant agreement indicate a desire to be helpful, or a strong desire not to be ravished any time soon?' he asked.

Claire shrugged and looked down. 'Both, I guess,' she replied.

'Hmmm. What's this new trick of yours of avoiding looking me in the eye? I've always thought one of your most admirable traits was your willingness to do exactly that when we talked, or yelled at each other. Is there something you're not telling me?'

'Certainly not!' Claire replied, jerking her chin free and trying to still the telltale quickening of her pulse. Why did the man have to be so blasted perceptive? She fixed him with an unflinching glare. 'Will you stop picking on me? I'm hungry, and I need to take a shower so I can have breakfast.'

'I hope food improves your disposition,' Terrill said, smiling wryly and standing. 'I had thought we might spend the day on the beach at Negril, but I don't think I want to take such a grouch along.'

Oh, dear, now I've overdone it, Claire thought glumly. She tried to smile sweetly. 'I'd love to go to Negril. Really, I'll be absolutely jolly once I've eaten somthing. I'm always cross when I'm hungry. You can ask my mother. When I was little she used to carry a packet of crackers along when we went on a trip, just to keep me quiet.'

'I'll tell Marisa to pack us a big picnic lunch,' Terrill said, his smile growing wider and more relaxed. 'Maybe I should call your mother and see if she has any other tricks for keeping you in line.'

'Get out of here,' Claire replied, picking up a pillow and throwing it at him. He flung the pillow back and left the room, laughing. Claire sat on her bed, clutching the pillow to her and burying her face in its softness. Terrill was so brave. Somehow, she was going to have to be, too.

CHAPTER SIX

'I DO think you ought to take at least a little interest in the hotel,' Claire said, frowning and trying to sound more cross than she felt as she looked down at Terrill, who was lying on a huge beach towel beside her, his eyes closed.

She had been so agreeable all day that she was afraid Terrill would become suspicious. She had let him take her hand as they walked along the miles of beach, admiring the swooping parasailors and the athletic windsurfers. She had got her hair braided again to please him. She had even willingly submitted to having him smooth suntan lotion on her back, a task he performed with such slow and leisurely delight that she was sure he knew what torture it was for her to lie as still as if his hand felt like any other hand to her. They had talked a great deal more about their lives before they had met, and Claire had at last learned a little about Terrill's short but illustrious career in professional football.

'I'm not sure I wouldn't still be playing if my back injury hadn't proved irreversible. It's hard to get used to an ordinary existence after having fifty thousand people cheering for you regularly,' he said, when Claire asked how long he would have liked to continue playing. 'I wasn't the least bit interested in settling down to a humdrum job.'

'I wouldn't say you had,' she replied. 'Did you really buy your first hotel on a whim, as they say in the stories I've read?'

'I really did,' Terrill replied with a boyish grin. 'I'd had an expert money manager all along, so I was in good financial shape. He thought I was crazy and would end up in the poor house. But when he saw I was serious, he helped a lot. I learned a lot of things the hard way on that first one. Mostly, not to be so gullible and trusting. Which is why I have you, my dear Claire. One of the reasons, anyhow.'

The gleam in Terrill's eyes as he said that made Claire uncomfortably aware of his other stated intention, to 'ravish' her. It was not, she thought, an appropriate time to encourage anything like that. For the present, she had to continue to act like that fish Terrill had mentioned. She would have to keep herself under very good control, not blurt out anything foolishly sentimental, if and when she did find the time right. As a result, she had decided to bring up the Jamaican Star, and see if she could get some answers to the mysteries that Ernest's revelations had earlier revealed.

'Well, you've handed me quite a job in the Jamaican Star,' she said, easing into the topic. 'The location is lovely, but I'd almost as soon start from scratch as try to fix up what's there. Ernest told me you wanted the land before the Melrose place was built. It's too bad you didn't get it when you first tried.'

'Maybe it's too bad I got it at all,' Terrill said, his expression suddenly withdrawn.

'Oh, no!' Claire said, afraid she had sounded reluctant to stay and work on it. 'I think it's going to be lovely, really. I'm looking forward to seeing what the architect has come up with, especially on the building where the main lobby will be. He said we can't use as much glass as I'd like because of the hurricanes, but he had some delightful ideas using extended beams and stonework. I don't think you'll recognise the place when he's through.'

'If you're trying to find out whether it's true, as I assume Ernest also told you, that I've never seen the place, it is,' Terrill replied, a forbidding tone to his voice. 'Nor do I want to any time soon.' At that, he had closed his eyes, and Claire had grumbled her complaint about his lack of interest.

'You can tell me about any problems you have and show me the architect's drawings,' he said, his eyes remaining closed.

Claire smiled to herself. Maybe a ghost would awaken Terrill's interest. She didn't want him to prowl around the hotel and help oversee the building process if it would be too difficult for him right now, but surely it wouldn't hurt him to take part with his mind.

'Well,' she said slowly, 'there is one little problem you might have some suggestions on, and I don't quite know how to draw a picture of it. It seems we have a resident ghost who sometimes walks the beach at night. Should we try to scare it away, or turn it into a tourist attraction?' She started to laugh, but the sound died at the sight of Terrill's face, pale as a ghost itself, when he quickly rose up on one elbow and stared at her.

'What ghost?' he demanded.

'Ernest said there was speculation that it was someone lost at sea,' Claire replied quickly. 'For goodness' sake, Terrill, you don't . . .'

'What did it look like?'

'I suppose like a sailor,' Claire answered, frowning. From the way Terrill had pooh-poohed ghosts when they were at the Rose Hall mansion, his reaction was the last thing she would have expected. 'What's the matter? You know as well as I do that there's no such thing as ghosts.'

'Of course not,' he agreed, giving an unconvincing little laugh before lying down and closing his eyes again. 'But if people think there's one, there might as well be. How did you think we might scare it off?'

'I thought maybe floodlights would do it. No one seems to see ghosts under well-lit conditions.'

'As I recall, those in Henry James' *The Turn of the Screw* appeared at all hours, even outside in broad daylight.'

'Yes, they did, didn't they?' Claire replied with a shudder. 'That story used to scare me silly. I hope our ghost is friendlier. Maybe we should give a prize to people who see it. Free drinks or something.'

'If we did that, the damn thing would be there all the time,' Terrill said grimly. 'Our liquor bill would be astronomical.' He leaned up again. 'Anyone seen this apparition lately?'

Claire shook her head. 'Not that I know of.' It seemed very odd that Terrill would be so concerned. 'Do you think it will be bad for business if the stories keep up?' she asked.

'Possibly,' Terrill replied. He stared out to sea for a few minutes apparently lost in thought, then looked back at Claire. 'Are you sure it looked like a sailor?' he asked.

There was something in his expression that sent a chill through Claire's body. It was haunted, almost as if he had seen the ghost himself. Perhaps it was the stress of his illness that made him more sensitive to thoughts of things beyond the grave.

'No, I'm not sure,' she replied, watching his face closely. 'All I know is that Ernest said people speculated that it was someone lost at sea. I suppose it coud have been almost any kind of person, even a pirate from long ago.'

'Or a woman,' Terrill said softly, staring past Claire as if he were seeing something even now.

'I guess so,' Claire murmured, but doubted that Terrill heard her. Why, she wondered, would he think of a woman? Had he perhaps heard something of a female ghost who walked the beaches? Something told her it would not be a good idea to encourage his thoughts along those morbid lines. She resolved to find out more about the ghost from Ernest. Maybe she would even spend an evening or two at the beach herself in hopes of encountering it . . . after Jayne arrived, as she was scheduled to do the coming week. Ghost-watching would be a lot more fun with some company. Not that she thought they would actually see anything, but just in case . . .

Now, however, it was time to get Terrill out of his moody state. It was so unlike that dynamic man to take something like a ghost so seriously. If it was his own problems that had led him to a sudden belief in the supernatural, it did not seem like a healthy direction for him to take. Far better that he go back to his new interest in her as a woman worthy of pursuing, no matter how limited his interest really was.

'Come on,' Claire said, getting to her feet and holding out her hand towards Terrill. 'Let's take another swim. It's been long enough since we had lunch, hasn't it?'

Terrill seemed to jerk his attention back from wherever it had been and suddenly focus on Claire again. With what seemed like a tremendous effort, he smiled brilliantly at her.

'Of course. Let's do that. Sorry, I got lost in a fog.

That ridiculous ghost story just reminded me of something that happened a long time ago.' He took Claire's hand and squeezed it, then pulled himself to his feet, stretching to straighten his back.

It was all Claire could do to keep from sighing in sheer admiration. Terrill Hawkes in a very small pair of trunks was a sight to make any woman sigh . . . even go into an old-fashioned swoon. Blue eyes, thick, dark hair, massive shoulders, slim hips, muscular thighs . . . it added up, Claire thought, to exactly what she would have ordered if she could have designed a perfect man. How could it possibly be that there was something terribly wrong? The thought made tears prick at her eyes. To hide it, she called out, 'Last one in's a rotten egg!' and ran for the water with Terrill close behind.

After almost an hour of frolicking in the water, they returned to the beach.

'This is the most absolutely perfect beach I've ever seen,' Claire said as she rubbed herself dry. 'The sand is so white, and the water so warm. I think I could become a real beach bum here.'

'Glad now that you stayed?' Terrill asked, lifting one eyebrow at Claire as he, too, towelled himself.

She smiled and looked away, her cheeks feeling warm. She couldn't very well deny it now, could she?

'I suppose I am,' she replied. But not for the reason that Terrill thought. 'Of course, starting tomorrow morning I do have to get to work, or the hotel won't get finished and your villa won't get redecorated.'

'Then how would you like to spend your last night of reprieve?' Terrill asked. 'Shall we go out and paint the town, or stay home?'

Stay home? It almost sounded like they were a pair, Claire thought ruefully. Well, in a way they were.

'Stay home,' she answered, slipping her beach robe on and picking up her bag. 'After all the sun and swimming, I'll be too sleepy for anything very wild.'

'Good choice,' Terrill agreed. 'I don't think I'll be a ball of fire tonight either, but if you wanted to go out, I'd go along. It is Marisa's night off, so there won't be anything for supper except what we do for ourselves.'

'After that huge picnic she sent along, I won't need much. But I can fix you some bacon and eggs if you get hungry.'

'Oh, so you *can* cook,' Terrill teased. 'I've never seen evidence of it before.'

'And you may wish you hadn't this time,' Claire retorted. 'My mother gave up trying to teach me.'

Terrill groaned, but later, as he sampled the results of Claire's efforts, he swore they were the best bacon and eggs he had ever tasted.

'I seriously doubt that,' Claire replied. In fact, she seriously doubted they were more than barely edible. Terrill had watched her with such unconcealed interest as she moved about Marisa's kitchen that she had become quite nervous. She had to snatch the bacon from the pan when it began to turn black in spots, and the eggs were entirely too well done to pass for 'over easy', as Terrill had ordered them.

For her own supper she nibbled on some pineapple she found in the refrigerator, and at the same time wondered anxiously if she was in for a replay of the previous evening. The tension was thick in the air, Terrill's eyes bright when he looked at her, the corners of his mouth quirking with a smile that seemed to promise that something besides a questionable plate of bacon and eggs was on his mind.

Claire returned one of those smiles briefly, and then looked attentively at her own dish of pineapple slices.

What should she do if he did try to kiss her again? She didn't want to cry and shout accusations at him. Nor did she want to appear to have suddenly taken the bait very willingly. He might get the impression that she had decided to let her passions take over from her mind and have a fling with him, like all of the other women he'd known, which was definitely not the case. But what impression did she want to give? Certainly not that she loved him so much she would gladly walk over hot coals for him. He would doubtless tire of such a woman very quickly. Surely there must be some middle ground.

She chewed on her knuckle and studied him, his angular face already quite tanned, his eyes shielded by dark lashes as he looked down at his plate. She wanted, she decided, for him to think that she gradually came to the decision to be his because of a genuine affection for him, combined with the physical attraction that he was already well aware of. She wouldn't declare her love and demand its reciprocation, but she would expect him to say some things that indicated he cared for her at least a little more than he had the other women in his life. What was it he had said that time in Palm Springs? That he wasn't looking for companionship? Well, she'd make him change his tune. No companionship, no sex. Period.

'Is that all you're going to eat?' Terrill asked, suddenly looking up and frowning accusingly at Claire's half-eaten little dish of pineapple.

Claire nodded. 'I'm not really hungry,' she said. 'I ate a lot of that chicken this noon.'

'And you'll be starving and cross as a bear by morning,' Terrill replied. 'Here.' He pushed the basket of toast towards Claire. 'Finish your pineapple and eat a piece of toast. I don't like skinny, sickly women.'

'And I don't like being ordered around,' Claire grumbled, but she picked up a piece of toast, slathered it with honey and then managed to down it along with the rest of her pineapple, while Terrill watched as if he were counting every bit. 'Now are you satisfied?' she asked, frowning, even though she admitted to herself that it was rather nice to have Terrill acting concerned about her personal welfare, since it was concern for his that had led her to tackle the chore of cooking for him.

'More or less,' he replied. 'Now, shall we have a nightcap out on the deck before we turn in? I don't like to go to bed right after eating.'

'Nothing for me, thanks,' Claire replied. 'I'll just look at the stars.'

Terrill grimaced. 'I probably shouldn't, either. It's a bad habit. How about a glass of milk instead? It's much healthier.'

Claire started to decline, then changed her mind. Perhaps Terrill's doctors had told him that drinking was bad for whatever his problem was. Good heavens, could he have kidney trouble? Something wrong with his liver? It didn't seem to her that he had ever used alcohol enough to cause such things, but her knowledge of such problems was very limited. In any case, she would henceforth do her bit to encourage more healthy refreshments.

'That sounds good,' she agreed. 'I don't think I've been getting enough calcium lately.'

'Very sensible,' Terrill said approvingly. He poured each of them a large glass of milk and carried them out to one of the tables on the deck.

They sat and drank their milk and talked about Jamaica, its beauty and the drive to promote tourism to help solve the persistent economic problems of the lovely island nation. The hotel would at least make a small contribution towards those ends. Terrill made no move towards her, and Claire's tension gradually diminished. At last she yawned, then smiled sleepily.

'I'd better turn in, so I can do some problem solving tomorrow myself,' she said, getting to her feet.

'I'll do the same,' Terrill said. As Claire started to turn and walk away, he laid a hand on her shoulder. 'Claire, please wait a minute,' he said softly.

Claire felt her knots of tension return, but she turned and looked up at him.

'What is it?' she asked, her voice husky.

'You know very well what it is,' he replied. With a hand on each of her shoulders now, he turned her to face him and looked down at her soberly. 'Why are you so afraid of me?' he asked.

'I'm not afraid of you,' Claire replied, the shakiness of her voice making her sound a liar. 'Not at all.' She studied his beloved face. Only so much in love with you that it hurts, she thought, and so worried about you I don't know what to do.

Their eyes held for what seemed like several minutes. Then suddenly Terrill's arms went around her and he crushed her against him, his cheek rubbing hers and his lips nuzzling around her ear.

'Oh, Claire,' he said hoarsely, 'I want you so much. What am I going to do?' He raised his head for a moment, his mouth quirked in a desperate little smile. Then, just as swiftly, before Claire could reply, his mouth found hers.

And I want you too, Claire thought, clinging to him, pressing against him, wishing that she could be this close, in the warm circle of his arms, for ever. She trembled as the softness of the lips she loved made her own feel like they had been awakened from a century's sleep. She loved the taste of him, the heady scent of him, the solid strength that felt at once so challenging and protective. She did not want him to stop kissing her, to stop the play of his hands that caressed her body so eagerly. Why should she? What were those silly thoughts she had had earlier? Oh, yes. She remembered now. She wanted more than desire to rule before she went further. She would have to back off once more but, lord knew, she did not want to. Her throat felt tight and tears rushed to her eyes as she pulled her head away.

'That's . . . enough, Terrill,' she said haltingly.

Terrill stared at her, bewildered at her tears.

'What is it, Claire? What's wrong? I know you want me as much as I want you. I won't hurt you. You must know that.'

'I know, but . . .' Claire swallowed hard. This was going to be much more difficult than she had thought. 'There's nothing wrong, Terrill. Nothing wrong with you. Just call me the world's champion prude if you want to, but I can't just hop into bed with you because we want each other. I've never done that sort of thing. I need time to think about it. I didn't have the sudden revelation you did that said everything was going to be different now between us. Please,' she pleaded, as Terrill continued to stare at her, 'just give me time to get used to the idea.'

'And how long do you think that might be?' he asked, frowning, his voice carrying some of its old harsh edge.

'I'm not sure,' Claire replied, anxiety replacing the warmth of moments ago. She did not want to have Terrill angry or disgusted with her. 'I just want to be sure why I'm doing it, if I do go to bed with you,' she said. 'It isn't enough for me to respond when my hormones come to a boil.

Terrill's mouth twisted wryly.

'I suppose what you're looking for is declarations of love all around?'

'Oh, no,' Claire said quickly, denying what was actually the truth as convincingly as she could. 'But I do remember that you once said you didn't even want companionship, all you wanted was sex, and I won't go for that.'

'Claire,' Terrill said, cocking his head now and studying her with a bemused smile, 'exactly what do you think we've had this past week if it isn't companionship?'

He did have a point there, Claire thought, smiling weakly in return. But she still wasn't ready to capitulate.

'I guess you could call it that,' she replied, 'but it has only been a week. For all I know, you've been suffering through it because you figured out that was the way to approach me. I need a little more convincing.'

'Damn it, I have *not* been suffering through it!' Terrill roared, thrusting Claire away and holding her at arm's length. 'I am not that kind of a devious phony! You know damn well I'm not!'

'Maybe not in business,' Claire replied, automatically matching his volume if not the harshness of his tones, 'but I've seen how you've treated other women. I don't want to add my name to the list of those that get fancy jewels and a note in six months. For all I know, you've been plenty devious to get them down the primrose path with you in the first place.'

'I never had to,' Terrill snarled.

'Well, maybe you're doing it now,' Claire snapped back. 'You are a very clever man.'

'And you are the most stubborn woman on the face of the earth!'

'I do believe you've mentioned that before!'

They stood stiffly still, glaring at each other. Then suddenly Terrill burst out laughing and pulled Claire back into his arms with a force that took her breath away.

'All right, Claire,' he said, his voice a soft rumble against her ear again. 'Take as long as you need to become convinced, but promise me one thing.'

'What's that?' she murmured, feeling her resolve begin to melt away.

'That you aren't simply stalling me off. That there will actually come a time, some time soon, when you will become convinced that I really do value your company.'

Claire smiled, letting her body sag against Terrill for the moment, her cheek nestled against his shoulder. She had won that battle much more easily than she had expected.

'I promise,' she agreed. And it would have to be quite soon. This holding back and pretending was exhausting.

CHAPTER SEVEN

CLAIRE plunged into her work with renewed energy. The promise she had made set her nerves tingling alternately with fear and excitement. She could sense that Terrill was watching and waiting, but he was never anything but companionable, even though his smiles seemed extra warm. From time to time he would touch her or plant a soft little kiss on her cheek. When she started and looked at him, he would raise his eyebrows and shrug as if to say it was nothing, really, for her to get excited about. But it was exciting, and she felt the excitement even when they were apart.

'You're looking absolutely super,' Jayne told her when Claire met her at the airport on Wednesday morning. 'Mr Hawkes must have been on his best behaviour lately.'

'Oh, he has,' Claire said. She had wondered how to tell Jayne that she now called him Terrill, and that he was staying away from the hotel, two things that anyone who knew Terrill Hawkes and the history of Claire's relationship with him would find very strange. She decided to tell Jayne that she had found Mr Hawkes so exhausted when he arrived that she insisted he stay at the villa and rest. In response to her mothering, he had begun to call her Claire, and she called him Terrill. 'But don't say anything to him about it,' Claire warned. 'You know how those macho types are about anything that looks like weakness.'

'My lips are sealed,' Jayne agreed. 'How long do

you think you can keep him quiet?'

'Heaven only knows,' Claire replied. 'So far, so good.' They loaded Jayne's suitcases into the 'smaller' car, which Terrill Hawkes kept at the villa—a large, if rather elderly, Cadillac. 'This is only the second time I've driven myself here,' Claire explained as they started off. 'Hang on. I woud have let Ernest bring the van, but I wanted a chance to talk to you alone.'

'Something else going on?' Jayne asked perceptively.

'Several things.' Claire told her about her encounter with Ben Williams and his cattle, then about the rumoured resident ghost.

'How neat!' Jayne exclaimed. 'I've always wanted to see a real ghost. Not that I believe in them. Can we see it, do you think? Does it only come by full moon, or what?'

'I have no idea,' Claire replied, 'but I'd like to go down to the beach and give it a try. I'm awfully glad you're so enthusiastic about the idea. I suppose it sounds silly, but I'd be scared to go alone.'

'I might be, too,' Jayne admitted. 'Well, when shall we do it?'

'How about tomorrow night? My parents are scheduled to arrive next week, and I'd like to do it before then. We're having you out to the villa for dinner tonight, so today we'll get you settled in the apartment Ernest found for you. It's a darling little duplex that belongs to your neighbours, a nice young couple who both teach at the high school. Then we'll find you a rental car, and give you a bit of a tour. There won't be too much for you to do for a while. The architect is just getting things moving, and the landscape gardener that's working with him the same. I expect there's some other correspondence for me to get caught up on, though.' She looked questioningly at Jayne.

'Quite a bit,' Jayne replied.

'Good. We'll use that as an excuse to spend tomor-row evening together. I don't want Terrill to know what we're up to. He's kind of funny about the ghost.'

'What do you mean, funny?'

'Well, he says he doesn't believe in them, but he acts as if it bothers him more than he's willing to admit. Of course, it may be just that he doesn't know quite how to cope with such things from a business standpoint. After all, it's not as if the Jamaican Star has any historical claim to fame that would entitle it to a traditional sort of ghostly presence.' Claire grinned suddenly. 'Maybe we should have it made to look like a creaky old mansion instead of a modern hotel. That might make it more acceptable. I'll suggest that to Terrill some time.'

Jayne laughed. 'I can imagine how that would go over with him. Well, we'll see what we can see tomor-row, but I wouldn't count on anything. Some friends and I spent days watching an old house that was supposed to be haunted near where I grew up, and never saw a thing except shadows. Chances are that's all anyone saw here. That and some mist from the ocean. Besides, if there is a ghost, it will probably stay away until the hotel is full of guests. If I were a ghost, I'd prefer to make a grand entrance and scare as many people as I could.'

'I expect you're right,' Claire agreed. 'It probably is a ridiculous waste of time, but somehow I just have to try it at least once. Maybe it's because I didn't have a haunted house to watch when I was younger.'

It was late afternoon when Claire drove Jayne to the villa for their scheduled dinner with Terrill Hawkes. Jayne had wanted to drive the little car she had rented, but Claire quickly scotched that idea.

'You'd better get some experience driving here before you try it at night. Ernest can bring you home.'

'It doesn't look so tricky to me,' Jayne said, making a sour face. 'All you do is lean on your horn and shut your eyes. Reminds me of New York City, except on the other side of the road.'

'Exactly what I meant,' Claire said drily, remembering the crumpled fenders on Jayne's stateside car. 'Now, prepare yourself to meet the new, relaxed Terrill Hawkes.' She, herself, was not relaxed. She was going to have to be on her toes all evening in order not to reveal anything of the new relationship between her and Terrill to Jayne, who knew her very well. And Terrill . . . she could only hope that he didn't hug or kiss her in front of Jayne. She had warned him not to, but the devilish smile he gave her when he'd seemingly agreed had not inspired confidence.

Terrill, however, was on his best, most charming, behaviour. The only fault Claire could possibly find was that his smiles were a little warmer than necessary, but she so adored being the recipient of those smiles that she would never complain. She noticed that Jayne was watching him speculatively, but Jayne was too tactful to say anything or even give Claire a knowing look.

'Well, how did I do?' Terrill asked when Jayne had left. 'Do you think she suspected anything?'

'I'm not sure,' Claire replied. 'I saw her looking at you suspiciously a couple of times.'

'Most women do that,' Terrill said drily. Then he took hold of Claire's hand. 'I don't want to spoil a pleasant evening,' he said, 'but I want to make something clear right now. I don't intend to play this game for very long. You promised . . .'

'I know, I know,' Claire said, pulling her hand away. 'I don't like doing it, either. Even though we haven't . . . you know, it still seems devious and stupid. But can you please just keep it up until my parents have come and gone? My mother would have a heart attack if she thought . . . well, if she knew. She's suspected for years that we're living in sin, to use her expression, but I don't think she ever really believed it, and I've certainly denied it as firmly as I could.'

Terrill chuckled. 'If I weren't so stupid, we would have been. All right, I'll do my best, but I consider that you've now set the date, so to speak. Agreed?'

Claire took a deep breath. 'Agreed,' she said breathlessly, and did not even complain when Terrill swept her into his arms and kissed her until her knees were wobbly.

The next morning Claire was sure that Jayne had picked up something of the electricity between her and Terrill, for she kept looking at Claire and smiling to herself. She said nothing, however, until they were on their way to the hotel after having had dinner in town, prepared for their evening of watching and waiting with dark clothing, blankets, and flashlights.

'So you and Mr Hawkes have finally realised you're in love,' Jayne said calmly, causing Claire to swerve her car and almost hit one of the ubiquitous roadside goats.

'Good heavens, whatever got you to that conclusion?' Claire asked, when her heart had quit thumping.

'It's as plain as the noses on your faces,' Jayne replied smugly. 'Oh, I suppose you'll deny it for a while, but you're wasting your denials on me. I'll just sit back and wait for an announcement of the wedding date.'

'I'm afraid the tropical sun has gone to your head,' Claire retorted. 'There is nothing going on between us that wasn't before. We're just . . . better friends, at least for the time being.'

'If you think I'll buy that, you're the one who's sun-struck,' Jayne replied. 'Besides, I'm perfectly willing to agree that nothing new is going on between you. I've known for ages what all of that thunder and lightning meant, even if you two haven't.'

Claire started to argue further, then silently pursed her lips and shook her head. Jayne was absolutely right, at least as far as she was concerned. Too bad she wasn't right about Terrill. She slowed the car, then turned in at the entrance to the hotel.

'Just going to check some measurements and then take a little walk along the beach,' she replied when the friendly gatekeeper asked what the two were doing working so late.

'Watch out for that ghost,' he replied, and then laughed heartily to show that he didn't believe in such things.

'It certainly is a pervasive rumour,' Claire commented. 'I wish we'd find out it's just some person who puts on spooky clothes and tries to frighten people. Otherwise it may never go away.'

'I wouldn't worry about it,' Jayne said. 'Most people will find it more interesting than frightening. You'd probably get more people coming in hopes of seeing it than would be scared away.'

'Could be,' Claire replied.

She parked the car near the building closest to the beach, which now had large piles of building materials and construction equipment beside it, waiting to be used. They got out and closed the doors silently.

'This way,' Claire said softly. She led the way to the

rocky end of the beach.

There were several places next to the steps which had been cut in the rocks from which they could see for a good hundred yards down the beach, once their eyes had become accustomed to the darkness.

'I'm glad we brought these blankets,' Jayne whispered, getting herself settled behind a jutting rock. 'These rocks are cold and hard.'

'I wouldn't want to do this every night,' Claire agreed, trying to find a place to put her flashlight where she could reach it. 'Maybe we should have waited until closer to midnight.'

'Let's hope this ghost can't tell the time and comes early,' Jayne whispered back. 'It's almost eleven o'clock now.' She peered around her rock. 'I sure can't see much.'

'The moon should be up soon,' Claire said. 'That will help.'

The two women whispered back and forth, taking turns keeping watch over the stretch of beach.

'I think we might as well go,' Claire said finally, when an examination of her watch by flashlight showed that it was a few minutes past midnight. 'At least it was a beautiful night to watch the moon on the water.'

'Shhh!' Jayne said, clutching her arm. 'Look. Way down the beach. Is that something coming?'

Claire squinted into the darkness. The half-spent moon cast undulating shadows from some windswept shrubs on to the shore, making it difficult to focus on one particular spot for long. In the distance, one of Ben Williams' cattle bawled and another answered, sending shivers down her spine.

'I don't see . . .' she began, then stopped. She *did* see something, something whiter than the sand in the moonlight. It was moving towards them with a strange dipping and swaying motion. Now and then it would pause and whirl around, seeming to expand as it did so. 'My God,' Claire croaked, turning to look at Jayne with huge, frightened eyes. 'What is it?' Jayne only shook her head and continued to stare at the apparition.

Closer and closer the ghostly white object came. It would rush towards them for a few moments, then return to the dipping, swaying and whirling. Claire's teeth began to chatter. Her heart was pounding. Her mind told her that what she was seeing was impossible, but she was seeing it. Jayne was seeing it, too. When the white shape had covered about half of the distance they were watching it paused, seeming to look around, but how it could was difficult to tell, for it had no eyes, no face at all. It was simply white, like a child draped in a sheet for Halloween. Then, suddenly, it let out an unearthly shriek and began moving swiftly towards them.

'Let's get out of here!' Jayne gasped, ghostly white herself.

Claire shook her head. She was not sure she could move if she wanted to, but she did not want to. There was a dreadful fascination in watching whatever it was resume its wild gyrations. She turned her head as Jayne plucked at her arm.

'Look,' Jayne whispered. 'It has feet.'

Sure enough, beneath what now appeared to be a filmy white garment, two small bare feet could be seen as the gauzy fabric flew outwards during a madcap whirl. The faint outline of arms could be seen, outstretched gracefully like a dancer. The motion stopped for a moment, then began again, except that one of the arms came from beneath the white veils, grasped one and flung it aside. A head appeared, with long blonde hair streaming out in the wind. Another veil was grasped and discarded, then another, while all the while the blonde girl danced on and on, graceful as a sprite, until all of the white veils were gone, and only a slender, bare, elfin girl remained, dancing madly in the moonlight.

'My God!' Claire whispered. She did not know why, but tears were streaming unchecked down her cheeks. It was no ghost at all, but only some poor, mad creature. She turned to look at Jayne, and saw that her cheeks were wet, too.

'What shall we do?' Jayne asked in a barely audible voice.

'I don't know,' Claire replied. She looked back at the girl, who was now slowing her dance, as if the music she alone could hear was coming to an end. In a moment she sank gracefully to the sand, holding a pose for a second or two and then lying down on her discarded veils. Then, abruptly, she sat up again, looking apprehensively down the beach in the direction whence she had come. Claire strained to see, then saw another sight almost more strange than the 'ghost'. A horseman was coming, at a gallop.

The sprite got to her feet, gathered up her clothes and clutched them to her. The horseman arrived, reining in his steed so abruptly that it reared.

'Damn you, Lorelei! Damn you!' the horseman shouted. He leaped from his horse, grasped the tiny woman around the waist and flung her across his saddle. Then he leaped back on to the horse, turned and galloped back down the shore.

'Ben Williams,' Claire said aloud. 'Good lord, if that isn't strange. Everyone thinks his daughter drowned.'

'Maybe he had more than one daughter,' Jayne said. 'Or maybe that isn't his daughter at all. Maybe it's someone he keeps imprisoned in that house of his, someone he keeps there for . . . his pleasure. You'd better tell Mr Hawkes. He'd know what to do.'

'No!' Claire said quickly, surprised at her own conviction. 'No, I don't think so. There's something going on here that I don't understand, but somehow I think there is some connection between that girl and the fact that Ben Williams called Terrill a devil. I don't think we should mention this at all—at least, not yet.' She did not want to tell Jayne that Terrill had asked if the ghost might be a woman, but she remembered very well the way he had looked when he did. As if he had seen it himself. Perhaps he had. Perhaps that had something to do with the other mysteries about Terrill Hawkes and this particular piece of property, and his reluctance to come here again, although for the life of her Claire could not imagine what it might be.

'You know,' Jayne said as they got back into the car, 'she was really quite an amazing dancer, and quite beautiful, too. How old do you suppose she is?'

'I have no idea,' Claire replied. 'It was too dark to tell. She reminded me of a movie I once saw about another dancer, Isadora Duncan. She used to dance with filmy veils like that, and she was a very strange sort of person. She died tragically, quite young. Do you suppose that poor creature thinks she is Isadora's reincarnation?'

'I have no idea what to think,' Jayne replied. 'All I know is that it's after one a.m. and I'm exhausted. Do we have to start in at eight in the morning?'

'Good heavens, no!' Claire said, laughing. 'This is Jamaica. We move a little more slowly here. Try ten o'clock. OK?'

Jayne readily agreed, and after dropping her off at her apartment Claire hurried back towards the villa. She was sleepy herself, the let-down after her fright having left her feeling limp and enervated. A soothing shower and a soft pillow sounded very appealing. But she had no sooner stopped before the wrought-iron gates to the atrium when Terrill Hawkes appeared, black brows drawn together in a fierce scowl.

What on earth was wrong with him? Claire wondered, watching as he rounded the car at a fast clip. He looked as if he were about to deliver one of his old-time harangues. When he jerked open the door and bent to deliver his glare at close range, then stuck his hand out towards her as if it were a bayonet, she was sure of it.

'Get out here,' he ordered loudly, grabbing her hand with a tight grip. When she did not move, he gave her arm a hard tug.

'Gee, thanks,' she said sarcastically, getting out as slowly as possible under the circumstances and frowning back at him. 'Charming welcome.'

He ignored her remark. 'Where in the devil have you been?' he roared.

'You let go, and stop yelling at me!' Claire shouted back.

'Shhh!' Terrill put his finger to his lips, apparently unaware of the incongruity of his request. He turned, still holding Claire's hand, trying to pull her along behind him. She dug in her heels.

'Stop it!' she commanded futilely, forced to move her feet or be pulled through the air like a kite. Only when they were inside the living-room of the villa did Terrill finally loosen his grip, simultaneously launching into a series of questions.

'What do you mean by staying out until this hour? Where have you been? I've been calling Jayne's apartment for hours. I was ready to call the police!'

'Call the police? Are you crazy?' Claire cried. 'I can take care of myself. I've been doing it for years. And I can't say I appreciate being greeted by the Spanish Inquisition when I get home.'

Terrill's hand tightened on hers again. 'You still haven't answered my question. Where in hell have you been for the last hour or so?'

'Out!' Claire replied loudly. 'Let go of me. You're hurting my wrist.' She finally jerked her hand free.

'Doing what?'

'Nothing!'

'That's no answer, and you know it!'

Claire jerked her chin up, breathing hard. 'I don't have to answer to you for every minute of my time,' she snapped. There was no way she was going to tell him any details of her bizarre evening. In fact, if he kept this up she would go out every night, just for spite. 'Jayne and I had a lot to catch up on, that's all. Now, if you don't mind, I'm tired. I'm going to bed. *I* have to get up and do some work in the morning.' She started to go around Terrill, but he stepped in her way. She looked up at him, frowning. He was frowning also, but deep in those beautiful blue eyes she saw real anxiety. Her heart melted. He had been truly worried about her. 'I'm sorry you were worried,' she said tightly. 'When Jayne and I finished our work, we went out for a little walk.'

'You shouldn't do that without a man along,' Terrill said, looking more anxious than ever. 'It isn't safe. Promise me you won't do that again.'

Claire made a face, although it made her feel rather comforted to have Terrill so concerned about her. 'Promise you this, promise you that,' she said, tilting her head and giving him a sideways glance. 'All right,

I promise,' she agreed, when he began to frown again. 'Next time I'll invite you to be our bodyguard.'

Terrill sighed in relief, his huge shoulders slumping forwards. 'I'll be happy to oblige.' He essayed a little smile. 'I'm sorry I yelled at you. I promised myself I wouldn't do that any more.'

'How else would I know it's really you and not some impostor?' Claire asked, smiling back. She really didn't mind it so much, now that she understood he hadn't just been trying to be bossy.

'Maybe we need a password,' Terrill said, a little glint of mischief finally relighting the sparkle in his eyes. He laid his hand along Claire's cheek, tentatively at first, as if he were afraid she would jump away, then more firmly when she did not. His eyes wandered slowly around her face, deeply intense and searching. They paused at her lips, then looked back into her eyes, full of a warmth that was almost tangible.

Claire held her breath, sure that he was about to kiss her and wanting him to more every moment. Then, suddenly, he looked away, withdrew his hand, shook his head, and swore softly.

'What's wrong, Terrill?' she asked.

'I don't dare kiss you tonight,' he replied, giving her only a brief glance. 'Goodnight, Claire.' With that, he turned and left the room, leaving Claire staring after him, bewildered. Did he mean that he wanted her that much, or was something else bothering him? Something related to his illness? Now feeling anxious herself, Claire trudged off to her room, her mind a scramble of questions about all of the things she did not understand. She was going to have to start finding some answers soon, before they drove her crazy.

CHAPTER EIGHT

'HE CALLED her Lorelei,' Claire muttered. 'If I could find out the name of his daughter . . .'

'*Miss* Forsythe! Are we going to get an office organised here or aren't we?' Jayne said, exasperated.

'I'm sorry,' Claire said, immediately contrite. Between worry about Terrill, who had behaved very strangely at breakfast, and the innumerable questions that plagued her about the encounter of the previous night, she had found it difficult to concentrate all day. She gave Jayne an apologetic smile. 'It's just that I'm so curious about that girl we saw. Now, where were we?' She tried to pay attention to the details that Jayne brought up, but her mind wandered off again. What if Lorelei was Ben Williams' supposedly drowned daughter? What if she hadn't always been the way she was now? What if there had been something between Terrill Hawkes and Lorelei, years ago? 'Yes, yes, of course,' she said, nodding, as Jayne asked her another question she had not heard.

'All right, I'll try it,' Jayne replied, her tone sarcastic, 'but I'm not sure a trained chimpanzee is exactly what we need to keep the books.'

'A trained . . . is that what you asked me?'

Jayne nodded.

'I'm afraid I'm not much good today,' Claire said with a sigh. 'You know what needs to be done as well as I do. Just go ahead and do it. Ask Ernest

119

where to find a bookkeeper. I think he knows every-one on the island.' And, she thought, he just might know the name of Ben Williams' lost daughter.

But when she asked him later, as he drove her home, he did not.

'They always kept to themselves,' he said, shaking his head. 'They came to this part of the island when his daughter was quite small. There were rumours then about his wife. Some said she had committed suicide. Others said it was sus-picious, that Mr Williams himself might have had a hand in it. You see, after that he seemed to have a lot of money, to buy the land here. But he didn't go out among people, even then, and no one saw the child except the few who visited him. When she drowned, there wasn't a regular funeral. Only a small item in the newspapers.'

'Then there was no investigation or coroner's report?' Claire asked.

'Nothing that I recall,' Ernest replied. 'Would you like me to enquire about it? My brother-in-law's nephew is the medical examiner now.'

'Oh, no,' Claire replied quickly. 'I was just curious about what had made the man so sour. It sounds as if he was always that way.'

'That's the way he has always seemed,' Ernest agreed.

At least, Claire thought, she had learned that there was only one daughter. Unless, of course, the warped Mr Williams had kept one completely hidden!

She had little more time to speculate about that mystery. It was, after all, a relatively minor concern compared to Terrill's health, which she feared was getting worse. He had been unusually quiet in the

morning, before she left for the hotel, his only
remarks a gruff 'good morning' and 'goodbye.'
Now, when she greeted him by the pool, he still
seemed nervous and irritable.

'Did you and Miss Cummings have a productive
day?' he asked, without looking up from his newspaper.

'Not especially,' Claire replied, hoping to get him
to at least look up and smile that beautiful smile of
his. 'I told Jayne to hire a trained chimpanzee to
keep the books, and she told me I was less help than
six thumbs.'

Terrill looked up, but did not smile. 'I didn't
know I was paying two clowns to work on my hotel,'
he said, as if disgusted by her remark. 'When I ask
an intelligent question I expect an intelligent
answer.'

'When you do, you'll get one,' Claire snapped,
her own nerves put on edge by Terrill's continuing
ill humour. 'Yes, we had a productive day. Things
will soon be running like clockwork. As usual.'

'Good,' Terrill replied, returning his attention to
the newspaper.

'Good,' Claire mimicked, throwing her arms up
in frustration. 'Isn't there anything else you'd like to
know?'

'No.'

A knot of anxiety formed in Claire's stomach.
Something was definitely amiss. If only Terrill
would talk to her about his troubles . . . but, from
the way he was acting, it was obviously not the time
to try to draw him out.

'I think I'll take a swim,' Claire said. Terrill said
nothing, and, when she returned a few minutes later
in her swimsuit, he was gone.

He did not reappear until dinner, at which time he was even more taciturn. He ate so poorly that Marisa fussed over him.

'Is there something else you'd like? Some nice ripe mangoes? A little ice-cream?' she asked hopefully.

'No, thank you.' He gave her a bleak smile. 'It's not your cooking, Marisa. I'm just not hungry.' He put his napkin on the table and nodded brusquely at Claire. 'If you'll excuse me,' he said, then got up and walked away towards his room.

'My goodness, that's not like Mr Hawkes,' Marisa said, watching him go with an anxious frown.

Claire felt so much like crying that all she could get out was a strangled little sound of agreement. Knowing something was wrong with Terrill was bad enough, but watching him disintegrate before her eyes was unbearable. She took her after-dinner coffee into the living-room and tried to calm herself by reading, but it was no use. She read the same paragraph over and over, making no sense of it at all, then simply sat and stared into space, trying to think what to do.

I've got to talk to him, she decided finally. She got up and went into her own room, leaning far enough out of the window to see that there was still light coming from Terrill's room. Then, feeling terribly shaky, she went and knocked on his door.

'What is it?' he asked gruffly, opening the door a crack. 'Oh, it's you.'

'Yes, it's me,' Claire replied. 'I've got to talk to you. Either come out here or let me come in.'

Terrill stepped into the hallway, closing his door behind him.

'What's the problem?' he asked, his face a stolid

mask.

'That's what I want to know. Can't you tell me about it?' Claire pleaded.

'There's nothing to tell,' Terrill replied. 'I'm simply trying to get in the right frame of mind for your parents' visit.'

Claire stared at him. 'That's no answer!'

'The hell it isn't. Don't be dense.'

Dense? Claire hadn't the faintest idea what Terrill was driving at. 'What has that got to do with your not talking to me and not eating your dinner?' she asked.

Terrill raised a sardonic eyebrow.

'Think about it, Miss Forsythe,' he said. 'Think about it. Goodnight.' With that, he opened the door and stepped back into his room.

Claire stood in the hallway, staring at the closed door, Terrill's words echoing in her head as if it were a huge, empty space. After a moment she turned and walked numbly back to her room, sat down on her bed, and tried to think. From what Terrill had said, it seemed he simply wanted to make sure he did not give their secret away by acting too affectionately towards her. He was trying to get back to their old relationship. But, somehow, that did not ring true. Why should that spoil his appetite? Why should he have to begin rehearsing it now? All he would have had to do was suggest that they go back to their former mode while Claire's parents were present, something they were both doubtless quite capable of doing after all the practice they'd had. No, Terrill was hiding something, and Claire was very much afraid that she knew what it was.

With a heavy-hearted sigh, Claire got up and undressed, took her shower, dried her hair, and then got into bed. She could not sleep. After counting two thousand, six hundred and fifty-seven sheep, she turned on her bedside lamp and looked at her clock. It was after two a.m.

'Maybe I should have a glass of milk and look at the stars for a while,' she muttered to herself. She got up, slipped into her warm pink velour robe, and went quietly to the kitchen for a glass of milk. With it in hand, she returned to the steps to the pool deck and looked out towards the sea. There, leaning against the railing, his back towards her, was Terrill, wearing a dark robe and slippers. Apparently he, too, was unable to sleep.

Claire hesitated for a moment. Should she sneak back to her room and leave Terrill alone to cope with whatever was bothering him, or try again to get him to talk to her? At just that instant, he suddenly pounded his fist against the rail and then dropped his head forward against his chest. Claire could stand it no longer. She flew across the intervening space and took hold of his arm. His head jerked upwards to look at her, and in the dim light she saw a look more desolate than she had ever seen.

'Terrill,' she pleaded, 'talk to me. It will help, really it will.'

'No!' he said, jerking his arm free with such force that the glass of milk in Claire's other hand sloshed over the rim of the glass. 'Leave me alone!' He turned and ran across the deck, took the stairs in one bound, and hurried back towards his room.

He's not putting me off this time, Claire thought grimly. She set her glass down and ran after him, arriving just in time to have his door slammed in her face.

'Let me in!' she shouted, pounding vigorously on

Terrill's door.

'Go away!' he yelled back.

'No, I won't go away,' Claire replied, even louder. 'I'll pound on this door all night if I have to.'

Terrill's voice next came from just the other side of the door, at a much lower volume.

'Claire, I will not let you in. Now, go to bed. You can't help.'

At those words, Claire felt as if her heart would break. She regathered her courage and replied, 'Yes, I can, Terrill. I care about you. You know that. And I know what's wrong. Please. Talk to me.'

'You can't possibly know,' he said, his voice softer still.

'Well, I do,' Claire insisted. 'If you let me in, I'll tell you how I found out.' There was no reply this time, and she held her breath, waiting hopefully. At last the door opened, and Terrill stepped aside while Claire entered.

'All right,' he said, standing stiffly before her and with his arms folded across his chest, 'tell me what you think you found out.'

Claire swallowed over the lump in her throat. 'I . . . I found out where you went before you came to Jamaica. The Mayo Clinic. I found the doctor's card in the telephone book that night I was going to leave. And the way you'd talked about changing your whole life-style because you might wake up some morning and find out you'd forgotten to smell the roses . . . I just put two and two together. I've been so worried about you ever since. I don't really know what they found out was wrong with you, but I . . . I know it must be something serious.'

Terrill stood silently, staring down at Claire. She stared back, feeling her heart pounding in her chest.

Was he angry? She could not tell. His face was completely impassive. Then his lips began to twitch. He chuckled for a moment, and then threw his head back and laughed until tears rolled down his cheeks.

'Claire, you're an idiot,' he said at last. 'There's nothing wrong with me except that same old problem with my back. I just went in for a thorough check-up. I'm in great shape.'

Stunned, Claire could only hear his words condemning her. Just because she had been worried sick, he had called her an idiot!

'I don't think it's funny, and I am *not* an idiot!' she cried. 'What did you expect me to think when you suddenly turned from a tiger into a timid little pussycat who wouldn't even go to the hotel? Something's wrong, and whatever it is, I hope it gets worse! You don't deserve anyone to care what happens to you, and from now on I certainly don't!' She whirled and stalked to the door, then turned back. 'As far as that promise I made goes, forget it! It's off!' With that, she went out and slammed the door viciously behind her, then went into her own room and slammed the door even harder and locked it. 'I don't care, I don't!' she said, flinging herself on to her bed and pounding her fist into her pillow. There was a loud knock on her door.

'Claire, I'm sorry. Let me in,' Terrill said.

Oh, so now he was sorry! Probably because he wasn't going to get her into bed, after all. Claire scowled and raised her head.

'No. Go away!'

The knocking was louder this time, as was Terrill's voice.

'Claire, damn it, let me in so I can explain.'

'Explain what?' Claire yelled back, sitting up and

glaring in the direction of the door. 'That you're callous and unfeeling except when you want something? Don't bother. I already knew that.'

'I am *not!*' Terrill's denial was accompanied by a punch at the door which made the walls shake. 'Let me in, or by God I'll break this damned door down!'

'Go ahead! It's your house,' Claire replied, but she got up and began moving slowly towards the door. Smiling grimly to herself, she remembered scenes she had seen in various movies. Silently, she unlocked the door and opened it just as she thought Terrill might be about to launch a full-scale assault. Instead, he was waiting silently, his arms folded. He raised one eyebrow and smiled.

'I thought you might try that,' he said, walking calmly into Claire's room. 'Good thing I know you so well, isn't it?'

'Too bad you do,' she replied. 'I'd have loved to have seen you go right out through the window.'

Terrill looked towards the window, smiled, then looked back at Claire.

'That might have really been bad for my health,' he said. Then his face became serious and he took Claire's shoulders in his huge hands, kneading them very gently as he went on, 'I'm sorry I laughed at you. It just seemed so incongruous that anyone could look at me and think that I was on death's doorstep.'

'Such things don't always show right away,' Claire replied, feeling a tightness growing in her throat. 'I had a friend once who had leukaemia . . .'

'I know,' Terrill nodded. 'It was stupid of me. I wasn't thinking. I didn't realise that you cared that much. Is that why you decided to stay and made that promise to me?'

Claire nodded, tears beginning to stream down her cheeks. They were tears of relief now. Terrill wasn't ill, after all. Terrill's arms came around her, and she flung her arms about him and buried her face against his chest, sobbing.

'What's the matter, sweetheart?' he asked softly.

'I—I'm just so glad . . . you're all right,' she got out between efforts to stifle her tears.

'So am I,' Terrill replied. He lifted Claire in his arms and then sat down with her on his lap on the edge of her bed. 'Dry your tears,' he said, handing her a tissue from the box by her bed. His arms tightened around her again. 'I'm not surprised you think that there's something wrong with me. In a way, there is, but it has to do with something that happened a long time ago and I have to work it out for myself. I'll start coming to the hotel this next week, I promise. But all of that has nothing to do with my decision to stop being a workaholic. That's just no way to live, and I definitely don't intend to be that way any more. I'd appreciate it if you'd help me on that. Bash me over the head, if necessary, if you see it happening.'

'Is that an order, Mr Hawkes?' Claire asked, smiling tremulously.

'It is, Miss Forsythe,' he replied, smiling back, his eyes deeply warm, and so clear that the blue seemed endless.

While he talked, Claire watched his face and thought over and over what a truly remarkable and wonderful man he was. But he still had not explained his earlier gruffness and lack of appetite. At the risk of ending this lovely, cosy moment, she decided to ask about it.

'You still haven't explained why you wouldn't

talk to me all day and didn't eat your dinner,' she said. 'I still can't see what that has to do with my parents' visit. If you want to go back to fighting while they're here, it's all right with me, but why go into rehearsal so soon?'

'Because,' Terrill said with a grimace, 'it's getting harder and harder for me to keep my hands off of you, and if I don't, there's no way I could wait until over two weeks from now to make love to you. Holding you like this is about to drive me crazy. But I won't hold you to a promise you made for the wrong reason. What I will do is extract another one from you, some time soon.'

'Oh.' Claire sighed and nestled her head against his neck, letting one hand reach up to caress his cheek and stroke his dark hair. She didn't want him to feel he had to wait longer because of her mistaken notion. She wanted him too, so much that her entire body felt the pleasant ache of longing now. 'You don't have to wait for my promise,' she said softly. 'I'll make it again, only just because I want to this time.'

'Oh, Claire!' Terrill's lips pressed against her forehead. 'That's very sweet of you, but I don't want that promise now. When I've worked out my other problem . . .'

'Can't you tell me what it is?' Claire asked, looking up at him anxiously. If only he would give her some clue that it had to do with Ben Williams and his daughter, she might tell him what she had seen and heard. But if it didn't, that bizarre situation might only distract him from the solution he sought. So far, he had not even mentioned the name of Ben Williams.

'No,' Terrill replied. He caressed Claire's hair

back from her cheek. 'It's something only I can face, and I plan to start doing so almost immediately. In the meantime, you'll have to excuse me if I get gruff and cranky and keep my distance. All right?' He loosened his grip on Claire and then lifted her off his lap.

'I guess so,' she replied dubiously, feeling suddenly lost and lonely without his arms around her. 'You won't even kiss me goodnight?' she asked in a small voice.

Terrill shook his head and got quickly to his feet.

'Not even just this once?' Claire persisted, following him to the door. She wanted desperately to feel his arms around her again, to touch her lips to his and drink in their sweet warmth.

'You sound like a child, begging for a lollipop,' Terrill teased, smiling down at her.

'Then humour me,' Claire said. She flung her arms around his neck. 'Just this once. I won't ask again,' she said. Her eyes searched Terrill's face. She could tell that he wanted to kiss her. His eyes were so dark, his lips so soft. 'Please,' she whispered, pulling his head towards her.

'God, Claire, don't do this to me,' he said, closing his eyes. Then they opened again, and his arms enfolded her, his mouth closing over hers with a hunger that left her breathless.

His lips moved back and forth with a fierce urgency that felt as if he were trying to devour her. Claire's head reeled at the knowledge of the depth of his passion. Her hands tightened across his back, her fingers digging in to hold him with every ounce of her strength lest she slip even one millimetre away from the pressure of his body against hers. Terrill's hands roamed her body, pulling her ever tighter to him, his arousal stimulating her own to a fever-pitch.

'Oh, Claire, I don't want to stop,' he groaned, burying his lips in the soft hair behind her ear.

'Then don't,' she whispered. 'I don't want you to.' She pulled her head back and gazed into Terrill's eyes. They were alight with a fire so strong, it seemed to burn into her own, igniting a new wave of longing that left her trembling.

'Are you sure this is what you want?' he asked, his voice strained but very gentle.

Claire nodded. 'Yes.' She clutched his strong neck as he swept her into his arms and carried her to the bed.

In seconds he had flung his robe aside and helped her remove hers. Then, as if she were as fragile as rose petals, he laid her down beside him. His mouth found hers again, more softly now, tantalisingly sweet and warm. She felt her body mesh against his massive form as his hands tucked her against him. On one side was the hard, passionate heat of his body, on the other were delicate caresses that felt like the beat of butterfly wings. It was a dizzying combination, and Claire heard herself making soft little sounds of pleasure, and the deep, low sound of Terrill's response to her own touches that explored him with a boldness that surprised and delighted her. Now she could feel for herself the taut muscles of the athlete's body that had for so long tempted her eyes. She wriggled and arched against him, wanting to feel his lips on breasts that felt swollen with desire. The message was understood, the resulting assault on tender, rosy peaks plunging Claire deeper into a maelstrom of sensations, calling forth, unbidden, a deep moan of desire. She not only loved Terrill, she wanted him far more then she had dreamed in her wildest dreams. Far more than she had known she could want any man.

Claire tugged at Terrill's shoulders, wanting nothing more in this world than to have him to cover her with his body, to make her his own. He raised his head, and the look in his eyes made her heart almost stop beating. They were wildly bright, dark with desire, yet misted and sad at the same time. Almost before he spoke, she knew what he was going to say.

'I can't, Claire. Not now. This is not the right time.'

With a violent thrust of one powerful arm, he pushed himself from the bed.

'Why not?' Claire cried, reaching towards him. 'What is it, Terrill? Did I do something wrong?'

'My God, no!' Terrill said, his voice harsh as he pulled on his robe. 'Except,' he added, frowning at her, 'getting me into that damned bed of yours in the first place. I can't explain any more. I tried to put you off, and I intend to do so until I've found the answer to my other problem. After that . . .' he smiled grimly '. . . you'll have one hell of a time getting me out of your bed.'

Claire clutched the sheet around her, feeling suddenly small and cold and lonely, her nerves racked by frustration. Was he only putting her on hold, or was he really putting her off indefinitely, like a parent telling a child 'maybe later' when what was really meant was 'never'?

'That's what you think,' she said sulkily. 'I don't intend to spend my life waiting for a fling with you while you try to get your psyche in order, or whatever you're doing. I'm twenty-seven years old, and I can't afford to wait much longer before I find a man who wants to get married and raise a family.'

Terrill paused by the door, looked back at Claire and grinned.

'Don't panic, old woman,' he said. 'Stick around. I think I may know just the fellow for you.' He went out, then poked his head back inside. 'And for God's sake, don't run any cold water for the next half-hour. I'm going to need it all.'

'Just the fellow for me? I'll bet you do,' Claire muttered as the door clicked shut behind him. She put her nightgown back on, got into bed, and turned off the light. She could still feel the warmth of Terrill beside her, still smell his scent on the pillow. Who did he think could ever take his place? She buried her face in the pillow, inhaling the essence left behind. There was no one, would never be anyone. Grim visions of an ancient, white-haired Claire Forsythe, tottering along with an equally ancient dog at her side, danced before her closed eyes. She would die an old maid, a spinster, unloved and unwanted. Except by her faithful dog. She would always have a dog. Terrill had wanted a dog. But he didn't want a wife. Or . . .

Claire suddenly sat bolt upright. He couldn't have meant . . . himself. Could he? She trembled, beads of perspiration breaking out on her upper lip. He might have. It was, just barely, possible. Oh, lord, if it was, she would be the happiest woman on the face of the earth. But she dared not get her hopes up. It would be too awful if she was wrong. Still, he had made so many changes lately. Almost as if he was planning to marry and settle down. But why wouldn't he tell her, if he was? What was it he had to deal with that would make him want to put that off?

Lorelei. It must have something to do with her. Why else would Ben Williams have such a hatred for Terrill? He must have loved her once, lost her, perhaps because of her father's insane possessiveness or jealousy. Now he thought she was dead. If that was it, what would he do when he found she was still alive and, apparently, quite mad, held prisoner by her equally deranged father?

Maybe that wasn't it at all. Claire rubbed her now throbbing forehead. She felt hope for the first time, but it was mixed with a terrible dread. She could end that dread, one way or the other, if only she had the courage to go to Terrill and tell him about Lorelei. But, like a patient fearing a dire diagnosis too much to see a physician, she knew she did not. She lay back down and closed her eyes. What could she do? Nothing. Nothing except try to get some sleep so that she would have the strength to watch and wait and wish that Terrill's problem and Ben and Lorelei Williams would all disappear like magic, and that she would wake up some morning and find Terrill in her arms.

CHAPTER NINE

'YOU'RE a worse mess today than you were yesterday,' Jayne commented drily, watching as Claire stood in the centre of the room, clutching a stack of file folders and staring vaguely into the distance. 'Did you and Terrill have a fight last night?'

'What? Oh, no. No. Everything's fine. Just fine.' Claire tried to smile brightly. 'I was trying to figure out what kind of welcoming party to have for my parents. They'll be here the day after tomorrow, you know. Terrill suggested we have a steel band come and play calypso and everything. What do you think?'

'Sounds terrific to me,' Jayne replied, eyeing Claire sceptically. 'You look as though you stayed awake all night worrying over it. Why is it I doubt you?'

'I can't imagine.' Claire plunked the file folders down on the new desk which had just been delivered. 'There. That's enough work for a Saturday, don't you think?' She looked around the room, actually a corner of the future lobby of the hotel, which had been walled off for them to use as a temporary office. 'Anything else I was supposed to do?'

Jayne sighed. 'There were those colour swatches from the batik company.'

'Oh, yes.' Claire picked up the pile of fabrics. 'I think I'll use this blue at the villa, and have the floor redone in white tile. That dark colour that's there shows every speck of dust and every footprint.'

'The villa?' Jayne cried, her eyes wide. 'Claire Forsythe, are you trying to tell me that you and Terrill Hawkes are engaged?'

'Good heavens, no!' Claire replied, but felt her cheeks turn scarlet. 'One of the first things Terrill asked me when he got here was if I'd fix up the villa along with working on the hotel. As you doubtless noticed, it's not very attractively decorated. It's still got the things the previous owner left behind.'

'Mmm-hmm,' Jayne said, cocking one eyebrow sceptically. 'Did you know, Miss Forsythe, that you are a terrible liar?'

'I'm not . . .' Claire began, only to be interrupted by a deep, familiar voice.

'So you've noticed that about her, too?' Terrill Hawkes stepped into the room, grinning mischievously.

Claire felt her blush intensify at the same time as her hands went clammy.

'How long have you been standing out there?' she demanded.

'Oh, about half an hour,' Terrill replied, his eyes still twinkling. 'Let me see that blue fabric.' He took hold of Claire's hand and looked at the piece which she still held. 'Very nice. And I like the idea of a white floor, too. Any ideas for the hotel?'

'Red walls with purple polka dots, and a green floor,' Claire replied crossly, her nerves tingling from the touch of Terrill's hand. If he was playing some kind of game, she did not appreciate it. If he wasn't, she wished he'd tell her.

'Sounds charming,' Terrill replied. 'How about adding some cacti with lighted spines in the corners?' He burst out laughing as Claire shot him a dark look.

'Private joke,' Claire explained to the mystified Jayne. 'It goes back to the Las Vegas hotel.' She retrieved her hand and looked up at Terrill. 'Have you had a chance to look around yet?'

'No. I thought maybe you'd like to give me the grand tour,' he replied.

'Of course,' Claire said quickly, finally beginning to recover from the shock of Terrill's entrance. It was going to be wonderful to have him working with her again. 'Do you want to come along?' she asked Jayne, hoping she would say no.

Jayne shook her head. 'I've got a date. My landlord's brother is going to try to teach me to windsurf this afternoon.'

'Have fun, then,' Claire said. 'I'll see you on Monday morning.'

She and Terrill took the architect's drawings in hand and went outside, looking each building over critically. They went through one of the buildings, one room at a time. Last of all they analysed the plans for the new lobby area. At each turn, Terrill had new and innovative ideas that improved on what had been planned.

'I'm certainly glad you decided to take part again,' Claire said when they had returned the drawings to her office. 'Everything will be so much better now.'

Terrill smiled, looking sheepish. 'Thank you, Claire,' he said. 'I don't deserve such praise, but thank you.'

Claire stared at him. For a while, she had forgotten that she was dealing with a different Terrill Hawkes. The old one would have taken her remark as only his due. It was rather unnerving, but very pleasant, to find that his changed character followed him everywhere.

'Would you like to look at the beach? The landscape man is planning some new terraced plantings at the rocky end,' she asked as they headed outside to his car. For just a moment she thought she detected a look of tension, almost fear on his face, quickly masked by a shrug and a little grimace. Was he still thinking about their ghost? Or was it . . . was it Lorelei? Of course! Why hadn't she thought of that before? He and Lorelei must have met here, perhaps as a trysting place. That could explain both his desire to possess this property and his reluctance to come here again. The memories were too vivid still, or had been until now, luring him back and yet repelling him.

'No. I'll wait until there's something to see,' he replied. 'Besides——' he smiled quickly, seeing Claire's anxious look '—we have an appointment at a beach resort in Ocho Rios. I know the manager there, and I thought we might pick up some pointers on running a hotel in Jamaica from him. After that, he's invited us to stay for dinner. Is that all right with you?'

'Oh, yes. That sounds wonderful,' Claire replied, still feeling a bit off balance. Terrill had always been reasonably polite, when he wasn't shouting, but mostly he had politely given orders. 'After that, we're staying for dinner,' would have been more his style.

They drove east along the highway which bordered Ben Williams' ranch. Terrill was broodingly silent, and Claire wondered what he was remembering about the sullen Mr Williams and his daughter. As they passed the gate, Terrill suddenly jerked a thumb towards it.

'That's the gate to our neighbour's ranch,' he said. 'Fellow named Williams. Not a very pleasant sort.'

For a moment, Claire thought of playing dumb and pretending she knew nothing of Ben Williams, but, having recently been told she was a terrible liar, she decided against it.

'I know,' she said instead. 'We've met.'

'You have?' Terrill was so startled that he swerved the car and then swore volubly. 'When?' he demanded, once the vehicle was back in control.

Claire explained about Ben Williams' wandering cattle, and her father's connection to Williams and his employee, omitting any reference to Williams' epithets about Terrill Hawkes. 'But,' she concluded, 'someone did fix the fence, so I didn't bother to mention it to you.'

'Must have been Hanover,' Terrill said, his expression grim. 'Williams is the most completely unreasonable man I've ever met.'

'I had the impression he's not mentally stable,' Claire said. 'Do you suppose . . .' she paused, wondering if she should go on, then plunged ahead, '. . . that it has something to do with his daughter's death?' Now, she thought, clenching her hands at her sides, I may find out some things I don't really want to know.

'He was always that way,' Terrill replied. He glanced over at Claire, his face a blank mask, but his voice deep with emotion. 'I knew his daughter, a long time ago. Her name was Lorelei. She was very beautiful.'

'Oh, I see,' Claire said softly. Yes, indeed, she

did see. Her speculations were being borne out, much sooner than she wanted them to be. Was now the time that she should tell Terrill what she had seen? She felt a sensation like a painful knife, twisting in her heart. Not yet. She couldn't. She bit her lip and cast a furtive glance at Terrill. To her relief, he took a deep breath, apparently trying to cast off the pall that thinking of poor Lorelei had cast over his mood, and then smiled at her.

'That's all water under the bridge now. I'm going to have to pay Williams a visit some day soon, but until then let's just forget about him. Would you like to stop at that little art gallery near St Ann's again? I had a notion that one of those paintings we saw might look good in the living-room at the villa, especially with your new blue and white colour scheme.'

'Yes, let's,' Claire agreed, trying to match Terrill's more cheerful look, but feeling that she was not doing very well. 'Which one did you mean? The one with the sea gulls?'

'That's the one,' Terrill replied.

They stopped and bought the painting, then went on to Ocho Rios. Their host was a genial man named Montoya, an enthusiastic fan of American football and, Claire gathered, of Terrill when he had played. While the two men alternately exchanged information about the past football season and the hotel business, Claire quietly sipped on a colourful drink topped by a tiny umbrella, and watched the windsurfers playing in the sea only a few dozen steps from the shaded patio where they sat. Soon she did not even try to follow their conversation, immersed, instead, in her own thoughts. How soon, she wondered, would Terrill pay his visit to Ben Williams?

Would he find Lorelei? What would happen if he did? And what would she do if he didn't? Simply tell him that she knew Lorelei was not dead, or describe what she had seen? If the latter, how in the world did you tell someone something like that?

'You've been unusually quiet today,' Terrill remarked on their way back to Montego Bay.

'Just tired, I guess,' Claire replied. 'I didn't get much sleep last night.'

'Neither did I,' Terrill said. 'Let's take it easy tomorrow and just lie around by the pool all day.' He chuckled and looked over at Claire. 'I'll bet you didn't think you'd ever hear me say that, did you?'

'No, I certainly didn't,' Claire agreed. 'I must say, I like it.' There was another thing she would like to hear him say, too. That he loved her and wanted to marry her. The tiny seed of hope that had been planted the previous night seemed to have grown, but it trembled with fear that having Lorelei Williams back in the picture would kill any chance she had of ever hearing those words. More and more, as she had thought about it during the day, she had become convinced that Ben Williams must have broken up a torrid love-affair between Terrill and his daughter. At the same time, she had become less convinced that Lorelei was really mad. Her behaviour had been bizarre, but could simply be the result of having been held a virtual prisoner by her father for so long. Perhaps the joyful shock of seeing Terrill again would bring about a miraculous recovery.

The next day, they did exactly as Terrill had suggested. Claire ploughed determinedly through a mystery novel, although she had trouble concentrating. Terrill was reading also, a dry-looking tome on the political structure of the early Grecian city states. he seemed withdrawn and reluctant to talk, leaving Claire to wonder whether it was because of her or because of his memories of Lorelei. Those were, she was sure now, the basis of the 'problem' he faced, although she was not sure exactly what problem still haunted him from that long past relationship, and why it apparently involved a visit to Ben Williams. By the end of the day she had resolved that, as soon as her parents' visit was over, she would tell Terrill about Lorelei. Until then, she was determined not to think about it.

Claire had Ernest bring the van to meet her parents at the airport the next afternoon.

'If I know Mother,' she explained, 'she will have brought enough luggage to stay a year.' Her expectations were correct.

'Well, I thought I might want to get dressed up a few times,' Mrs Forsythe said defensively when Claire teased her about the number of suitcases. 'Didn't you say Mr Hawkes is having a party for us tonight? There, you see . . .'

'But we won't be dressed up for that,' Claire said patiently. 'Wear some slacks and a pretty top. Mr Hawkes has hired a calypso band, and you might want to give the limbo a try. Everyone does.'

'That I've got to see,' Roger Forsythe commented drily. 'The last time your mother did anything like that was when she was a cheerleader in college.'

Once the elder Forsythes were settled in their rooms, Claire took them for a walk along Doctor's Cave Beach. The many vendors, selling everything from mahogany masks to conch shells, soon had her mother in what her father called her 'buying frenzy'.

'You'd better hold her back,' Claire told him.

'There's a crafts market the other side of town that will drive her wild.'

'Let her go,' her father said benevolently. 'It's been a long, cold winter in Illinois.'

'How is your research going?' Claire asked. She was wondering if, for a change, he was really going to take some time off. On that would depend how eager he was to see his former student, someone he could discuss his research with. The problem of how she should bring up the topic of Ben Williams, and how much she should tell her father about the man's peculiarities, had been troubling her. It was possible the man might be completely reasonable when talking to her father. It seemed equally possible that he might, given the fact that he knew she worked for Terrill Hawkes, launch into some kind of maniacal tirade.

'Very well,' Roger Forsythe replied. 'I've got some new data that I know Harold Hanover will be very interested in.'

'That's nice,' Claire said, her heart sinking. 'Well, when you want to go and see him, just give Ernest a call. He's going to be at your disposal while you're here.'

Roger Forsythe frowned. 'I thought I'd rent a car. I've never driven on the left, but I think I can handle it.'

'Don't try it,' Claire advised. 'They use a whole different technique in Jamaica. At least, ride around with Ernest for a while before you do, so you can see what I mean.' She hoped that doing so would discourage her father, who was the quintessential absent-minded professor behind the wheel of a car, given to moments of meditation during which he seemed oblivious to his surroundings.

'Oh, just look at those pretty necklaces,' Mrs Forsythe said, heading for a small boy who was holding some up hopefully.

'Come on, Mother, you'll see a million more,' Claire said. 'Why don't you go back to your hotel and take a rest now? I'll go on back to the villa, and send Ernest for you at about six o'clock.'

'All right,' Mrs Forsythe said reluctantly. 'Oh, but he's so cute.' She hurriedly purchased a necklace, giving Claire a defiant look. 'Now I'll go back to the hotel. Are you sure I shouldn't put on a party dress for tonight?'

'Yes, I'm sure,' Claire replied. She escorted her parents to their room, then went back to the villa, where Marisa had preparations for the party well under control. Terrill was nowhere in sight, so she showered and dressed for the party in slacks and a batik print top she had bought for the occasion. Then she wandered out to the pool deck and paced restlessly back and forth. The thought of her parents meeting Terrill for the first time had her insides tied into knots. She wanted them to like him. She wanted them to love him. But she didn't want them to suspect that their relationship was anything but friendly. Which, after all, it might not be. It seemed a hopeless combination. She leaned against the railing, staring out towards the bay, but seeing nothing but Terrill's beloved face. Why, oh, why did everything have to be so complicated? Why hadn't she just stayed home in Illinois, had a nice, quiet life, and married some ordinary young man? Why hadn't she listened to her mother?

'Shall I call you Miss Forsythe tonight?' Terrill asked, coming quietly up beside her.

'Good lord, you startled me!' Claire said, recoiling

and looking up at Terrill, her heart lurching into a fast pace. He looked even more wonderful in reality, the blue of his eyes vivid against his deep tan.

Terrill smiled, that special, warm smile that Claire loved. 'You seem a bit tense. If it will make you feel better, I'll even pick a fight with you.'

Claire shook her head. 'No, thanks. I don't think I'm up to fighting back. Let's go ahead and call each other by our first names. It seems too unnatural not to any more.'

'I agree,' Terrill replied. 'Now stop worrying. I'll be equally charming to you, your mother, Mrs Montoya and Jayne.' He loosened Claire's hand from its grasp on the railing. 'Good heavens, Claire, your hand is like ice. Calm down! Everything is going to be fine. Let's have a cup of rum punch right now, before you tie yourself into any more knots.'

'No, thanks. I'd fall flat on my face,' Claire said, heaving a sigh. 'I'll be all right.'

'Do as I say,' Terrill said firmly. He led Claire to a chair, then brought them both a cup of punch. 'To Dutch courage,' he said, raising his cup before taking a drink. He smiled warmly again as Claire reluctantly sipped hers. 'Sometimes it takes a little something extra to face a *bête noire*. Then again, sometimes all it takes is the old-fashioned kind of courage. You know, Claire, I think that I may be able to explain what's been bothering me far sooner than I thought I would. I think my particular *bête noire* has grown far larger in my imagination than it is in reality. And when mine is vanquished, yours will be too.'

'You're talking in riddles,' Claire complained. 'I don't have a *bête noire*.' More like a couple dozen of them, she thought grimly.

'Come now, Claire, you're being dense again,' Terrill teased. Then he raised his head, listening. 'I think I heard the van. Time to become the perfect host.' He put on a silly grin and slicked his hair back. 'How's that?' he asked.

'Perfectly awful,' Claire replied, giggling in spite of herself. 'You look like a confidence man about to steal money from an old lady.'

'That's the real me,' Terrill said. 'Vulture Hawkes, they call me. Come on and introduce me to your parents. Be sure and tell your mother to watch her purse at all times.'

Claire was laughing so hard that she had trouble making the introductions, but somehow Terrill's trick had worked magic on her tension. The rest of the evening went off flawlessly. As promised, Terrill was equally charming to all of the women, quickly casting a spell over Mrs Forsythe that had her beaming happily at Claire, instead of watching with the narrow-eyed suspicion Claire had feared. He was equally adept at finding a common meeting ground with Roger Forsythe and with Jim Raines, the young landlord's brother, who accompanied Jayne.

'His football background makes it especially easy for him to relate to all kinds of men,' Mr Forsythe remarked to Claire in his usual analytical way. 'I like him. I think you've found a fine man there.'

'Daddy, we are *not* romantically involved,' Claire protested, surprised at the remark. It was more what she would have expected from her mother.

'Well then, you should be,' he retorted. 'Men like him are hard to find.'

Claire made a face at her father, at the same time

thinking how very right he was.

'How did I do?' Terrill asked, when the last guest had departed.

'I'd give you top grades,' Claire replied. 'Mother was as happy as a cow knee-deep in clover, and my father thought you were terrific. He even said so.'

'Thank God,' Terrill said, sinking into a lounge chair with a heavy sigh. Only then did Claire realise how hard he had been trying, for her sake, to make the right impression.

'I really appreciate your efforts,' she said. 'It makes life a lot easier for me.'

Terrill smiled, his eyes twinkling with mischief, but he did not reply to her thanks. Instead he said, 'Spend as much time as you want with them while they're here. I want to keep up my image.'

'I expect I'll have to take Mother shopping a lot,' Claire replied. 'My father's apt to go off looking for cattle people to talk to every chance he has. He's planning on getting in touch with Harold Hanover tomorrow.'

But, on the following day when Claire arrived at her parents' hotel to take her mother on a shopping expedition, her father reported that a call to Harold Hanover's telephone number produced the information that his telephone had been disconnected.

'That's odd,' Claire said, frowning. 'I talked to him a few weeks ago. Maybe he's moved. Do you know where he lived?'

'I have his address somewhere,' her father replied. 'I hope I remembered to bring it with me. I didn't expect to need it.' He searched through his briefcase full of papers, sighing in frustration when he did not find the needed address. 'Oh, well,' he said, with a regretful smile, 'I expect Ben Williams will know where he's gone. I'll have Ernest take me to his place tomorrow. It isn't far from here, is it?'

'No, but . . .' Claire bit her lip. What should she say about Ben Williams?

'But what?' Her father eyed her closely. 'Harold did work for him, didn't he?'

'Yes,' Claire said, 'but Mr Williams is a semi-recluse. He doesn't see anyone at his house. It supposedly stems from the time when his daughter drowned some years back. Anyway, if I were you, I'd call first.'

Her father nodded. 'I'll do that. Meanwhile, I'll have Ernest take me to see a fellow I know who raises cattle a little further down the coast. I have the map he sent me of how to get there.' He brandished a sheet of paper. 'You girls have a good time shopping. Just remember to leave a few things for the other tourists.'

'Oh, Roger!' Claire's mother scolded, but by the time they returned to the hotel, Claire was afraid his warning had been fairly accurate.

'How will you ever get everything home if you keep this up?' Claire asked.

'In boxes, I guess,' her mother replied vaguely. 'Remind me to look for some.'

'I'll ask Marisa where to find some,' Claire said, shaking her head. It might be more to the point to ask her mother if she was planning on adding a room to their house to display all of her acquisitions, but she was afraid she might start an idea brewing that her father would not appreciate. 'Let's go down to the terrace and wait for Daddy,' she suggested. She did not especially want to be present when her father saw the mountain of purchases from just one day's shopping.

Claire and her mother had only just begun to sip

tall, cool glasses of iced tea when her father and Ernest appeared.

'It is very strange, Miss Forsythe,' Ernest reported immediately. 'On the way to the other ranch, I noticed that the gate at the Williams ranch was shut. We stopped on the way back. It is not only shut, but padlocked. Nor did we see any cattle.'

'That *is* odd,' Claire said, feeling a shiver of apprehension. Everything connected with Ben Williams seemed to have an aura of the bizarre about it. Not that she would be sorry to find that he and his cattle and his daughter had disappeared from the face of the earth. 'Maybe he's gone on a trip,' she suggested.

'Cattlemen can't just pick up and leave on trips, and you know it,' her father replied. 'I'm going to our room and try his telephone immediately. I can't believe the man's disappeared too, along with a couple of hundred cattle.' In a few minutes, he returned, shaking his head. 'No answer. But at least I didn't get a message that the telephone had been disconnected.'

'I shall make enquiries about Mr Hanover,' Ernest said. 'I will surely find someone who knows where he is, or at least where he has lived until recently.'

'And in the meantime,' Roger Forsythe said, 'I'm going to try a little snorkelling, and then later in the week Ernest will drive me to see a ranch near Kingston.'

For the next few days, Claire had a feeling of suspended animation, almost as if she were holding her breath for news of the vanished Harold Hanover, and the still absent Ben Williams. Terrill's behaviour added to her tension. He seemed distraught over the sudden absence of Ben Williams, as if some key to the final solution of his problem had suddenly been taken from him. It did not help when Ernest came up with an address for Harold Hanover, a small house in the neighbouring town of Falmouth. He and Roger Forsythe went there, only to discover that the man had moved out during the night about ten days previously, leaving no forwarding address.

'Something is definitely wrong,' Terrill said, frowning, on hearing that news. He and Claire had joined her parents for dinner at their hotel.

'Do you suspect foul play?' Claire's mother asked, wide-eyed. 'Perhaps we should notify the authorities.'

'Now, now, Mother, don't get excited,' Roger Forsythe said soothingly. He turned to Terrill. 'I'm going to drive up to the research farms near Montpelier tomorrow. I'll see if anyone there knows anything about either Williams or Hanover. If not, why don't you and I go over the fence the next day and poke around at the Williams spread?'

'Good idea,' Terrill agreed, sending Claire's heart right into her throat. Heaven only knew what they might find there.

She was so nervous the next day that, after a picnic lunch which she and Terrill had eaten on the beach in front of the hotel, he gathered her into his arms and kissed her for the first time since her parents' arrival.

'What was that for?' she asked, trembling from a whole new set of sensations, but for the first time finding little comfort in the warmth of Terrill's embrace.

'I thought you needed kissing,' he replied. 'God knows, I do. We're both wound up like clock springs, though I'm not sure why you are.'

'I'm worried about Daddy's driving to Montpelier by himself,' Claire replied, which was, at least, partly true.

'Why?' Terrill persisted, brushing her hair back

from her forehead and kissing her there. 'He's a responsible driver, isn't he?'

'Most of the time,' Claire replied with a sigh. 'It's the times when he isn't that bother me.'

'He'll be fine,' Terrill said comfortingly, treating Claire to a dazzling smile.

She smiled back, suddenly feeling nothing more than an overwhelming desire to kiss Terrill again. She flung her arms around his neck and did so, her heart soaring at the passion with which he responded. He did love her. He must. And oh, how she adored him!

She and Terrill puttered about the hotel all afternoon, Jayne having volunteered to take charge of escorting Claire's mother on a tour of some of the tourist attractions. They discussed the landscaping, which was now in progress, then strolled idly along the beach.

'This is the very first place that I went into the ocean in Jamaica,' Terrill said, flipping a rock into the water and watching it splash. 'It was right after I bought the villa. Someone told me it was a nice, uncrowded beach. There wasn't any hotel here then. Just an old fisherman's shack.'

'It still is a lovely beach,' Claire said, watching Terrill's face closely. There was no sign of sadness, only a very thoughtful look. Was he thinking of Lorelei? Would he, at last, say more than that he had known her?

'Except for our ghost,' Terrill said, smiling wryly at Claire, as if he now thought the idea ridiculous.

With a great effort, Claire tried to keep her own expression from showing the inner turmoil which his casual remark had caused.

'Yes, except for that,' she agreed. 'But no one's seen it lately. I expect it was just someone's overactive imagination.' She felt guilty about her prevarication, but what else could she say? That it wasn't really a ghost at all, just Lorelei Williams dancing in her white veils? That revelation would destroy Terrill's new found calmness at the spot where, she guessed, he and Lorelei had spent a lot of time, perhaps . . . perhaps made love.

'Or something they'd been drinking or smoking,' Terrill replied with a meaningful lift of one dark brow.

Claire nodded. 'Quite likely.' She took a deep breath and tried to smile brightly. 'Too bad we don't have our swimming suits. Maybe we should bring them tomorrow.'

'Let's do that,' Terrill agreed. 'Well, shall we go back to the villa and have a swim in the pool before dinner? You can call and check up on your father, too, and ease your mind.'

But, as soon as they arrived at the villa, Claire was greeted by Marisa with word that her mother was, that very moment, on the telephone, sounding very distressed.

'Your father's been in a wreck!' Mrs Forsythe blurted the moment Claire answered. 'He's not badly hurt, but he demolished the rental car, and there are police and reporters all over the place.'

'Oh, no! Where are you?' Claire cried, clutching at Terrill's arm. At his questioning look, she put her hand over the receiver. 'Daddy's been in a wreck,' she told him. 'Where?' she repeated, trying to make sense of her mother's rapid speech. 'Yes, Mother, we'll be right there.' She looked at Terrill and shook her head. 'What did I tell you?' she said. 'He's at the hospital emergency room, but I couldn't make much sense from anything else Mother said, except he's not badly hurt.'

'Let's go,' Terrill said, putting his arm around Claire. In record time he had them at the hospital, and it was no problem at all to find Roger Forsythe. Doctors, nurses, and policemen were milling around in the hallway outside a room where he was sitting on an examining table, a bandage around his head, but otherwise in fine spirits, fielding questions from a young reporter.

'Must be a slow news day,' Claire commented drily, when she had hugged her still upset and excited mother.

'That is not it,' replied one of the policemen, who overheard her. 'My cousin Ernest has told me of the famous scientist, Roger Forsythe, and when I got the call that he had been in an accident, I telephone the newspaper.'

Claire almost burst out laughing, in spite of her mother's anxiety. The ubiquitous Ernest again. When the officials and newsman had left, Claire at last had a chance to ask her father what had happened.

'I was driving along a little country road near Montpelier,' he replied, 'when suddenly this boy riding a donkey appeared from out of nowhere, right in front of me. Naturally, I didn't want to run into them, so I went into a ditch instead. Turned out to be a pretty deep ditch, and very rocky, or I'd have been able to get back out.'

'Poor darling,' Claire said, giving her father a comforting hug and kiss. She knew it would do no good to tell him that boys riding donkeys did not appear like magic, and that he probably had had his mind a million miles away just before he saw them.

'Did you find out anything about Williams and Hanover?' Terrill asked, once they were comfortably seated in his car and on the way back to the Forsythes' hotel.

'Nothing relevant to the present situation,' Roger Forsythe replied. 'I did find out that Williams got into trouble about five years ago for trying to bring a prize bull into this country illegally.'

'Good heavens!' Mrs Forsythe exclaimed. 'How could you smuggle something as large as a bull?'

'It wasn't exactly smuggling, Mother,' her husband said patiently. 'He tried to bribe some officials to pass it without the proper inspection and quarantine procedures. He pleaded *nolo contendere* and paid a large fine.'

'That doesn't surprise me,' Terrill said grimly. 'The man's always felt he was a law unto himself.' At Roger Frosythe's questioning look he added, 'I've dealt with him before. Well, shall we have a look around his ranch tomorrow? There may be nothing to see, but I'm getting very curious. I tried his number today and there's still no answer.'

'Dear, you shouldn't . . .' Mrs Forsythe began, but her husband interrupted quickly.

'I'm certainly game. But if we don't turn up something, we'd better notify someone, don't you think?'

'Definitely,' Terrill agreed. 'If we don't find something, or someone.'

'I'm coming with you,' Claire announced firmly, although her nerves were taut at the very thought. She felt morbidly like a criminal planning on returning to the scene of his or her crime. She wanted to be there when Terrill and her father discovered whatever there was to discover. If there was nothing, she knew she would have to tell what she knew. But if there was . . . she did not want to think about that possibility.

CHAPTER TEN

'CLAIRE, you are *not* coming along!' Terrill Hawkes roared the next morning when she reiterated her intentions.

'Oh, yes, I am!' Claire shouted back.

'Claire, be reasonable.' Terrill's voice was wheedling now. 'It might be dangerous. Williams is, as you said, quite unstable. If he's there, God only knows what he might do.'

'All the more reason for me to come,' Claire persisted. 'You and Daddy might need someone to go for help.'

Terrill sighed. 'You, Claire Forsythe, are the world's most stubborn woman.'

'So I've heard,' she replied. 'Let's go.'

They were starting to get into the car when Marisa appeared at the doorway of the atrium.

'Mr Hawkes,' she called, 'Mr Forsythe is on the telephone for you. He says it's important.'

'I wonder what that could be about?' Claire said, following Terrill back inside the villa.

Terrill shrugged and went to answer the telephone. He appeared again a short time later, shaking his head.

'Our excursion is off,' he said to Claire. 'Your father just got a call from Ben Williams. They're meeting for lunch in town. It seems Williams saw the article about your father's accident in the morning paper.'

'If that isn't the darndest thing,' Claire said, feeling

a sudden let-down at the news. She had had herself primed to face whatever she might have to face when Terrill found out that Lorelei was still alive. Now, it seemed, she had to wait again. 'Well, maybe now we'll find out what happened to Harold Hanover.'

'Could be,' Terrill replied. 'I told your father we'd come down to their hotel at about three o'clock and get his report.' He smiled wryly. 'I had to warn him not to mention my name. Old Williams doesn't think much of me, I'm afraid.'

That, Claire thought, was putting it mildly, but she said nothing about the violent reaction she had received from Ben Williams on the mention of Terrill's name. 'What shall we do in the meantime?' she asked instead. 'There isn't really anything at the hotel that needs attention right now, and I'm still waiting for the estimates on the new floors for the villa.'

'We talked about going swimming at the hotel beach,' Terrill said. 'Why not have Marisa pack us a picnic again and do that? We can go right to your parents' hotel from there.'

'That's a wonderful idea,' Claire agreed. Maybe being with Terrill in the bright tropical sunshine would erase the feeling of foreboding that still seemed to hang over this day.

They had the beach to themselves. Terrill seemed perfectly relaxed and happy, as if he had now completely overcome the shadowy memories the beach had held for him. He and Claire swam out to a reef, rested for a while, then swam back and ate their lunch. Afterwards, Terrill asked Claire to spread lotion on his back, a task she found so stimulating that she kept smoothing her hands across his broad shoulders for far longer than necessary.

'I do believe you're enjoying that,' he teased, turning his face up to smile at her.

'I do believe you're right,' she answered. 'How about doing my back now?' She almost purred in pleasure at the touch of Terrill's hands, wondering how anyone so huge could be so gentle. When he had finished he lay down close beside her and put an arm around her.

'I think I may as well tell you why I avoided this place at first,' he said. 'I'll be able to see Williams soon, now that he's surfaced again, and get the last bit off my chest then.'

Claire felt her stomach go into a knot. She wanted to cry out, 'No! Don't! I know something that may change everything!' but the words stuck in her throat. She could only stare into Terrill's beautiful blue eyes and listen silently.

'I met Lorelei Williams here, on this beach,' he said, stroking Claire's hair back from her face as he spoke. 'It was the second time I'd come here to swim. She came riding along on a big white horse, like some angel in a dream, her long blonde hair streaming out behind her. She seemed startled to see me here, and turned and rode off immediately, ignoring my calls for her to stay. I came back day after day, hoping to see her again. Finally she came back, and this time she stopped. She got off her horse and came over to me. She was a tiny thing, light as air. She spoke so softly, I could barely hear her. She told me her name and said she lived with her father downshore, and that he never let her go out. We talked for a while, but she said she couldn't stay. I wanted to see her again, so we arranged to meet here at night. She said she often slipped out, and her father didn't know. So, we met that night, and for many nights thereafter. Sometimes she was so sad, telling me she wondered if she wanted to live on as she had to with her father. Other times, she told me of her dreams of being a dancer, and would dance for me, as wild and free as a bird. I told her of all the wonders of the outside world she'd never seen, and she begged me to take her away so that she could see them. It was like a fairy-tale, really. I was so much in love that I could hardly stand it, and, I guess, it didn't occur to me that I was getting involved in something I couldn't handle.' He paused and sighed deeply.

'What do you mean, couldn't handle?' Claire asked.

'Her father. After our first few meetings, Lorelei and I began making love. She was the most passionate creature I've ever met, almost insatiable, especially when she'd been dancing. Then, one night a couple of months later, her father caught us. He was, putting it mildly, enraged. He even threatened to kill me if I ever tried to see Lorelei again. I tried to reason with him, but it was no use. I banged on the door and got a shot-gun blast over my head in reply. I saw a lawyer, but there was nothing anyone else could do. If a father chooses to keep his daughter a prisoner, that is his right, as long as there's no evidence he mistreats her. The few people who had seen Lorelei said she never complained. At last I had to go back to the States to start the football training season, but I thought of Lorelei constantly, laying plans as to how I was some-how going to sneak back in and kidnap her. I even wrote to old Williams and told him that if he thought he could keep Lorelei and me apart he was crazy.'

All the while Terrill was talking, Claire's heart kept pounding, telling her over and over that she must tell him now. At last she could keep silent no longer.

'Terrill, there's something . . .'

'Shhh!' He placed his finger on her lips. 'Let me finish. It was in December that I got an envelope from Jamaica. It was from Ben Williams. All it contained was a clipping from the newspaper, saying that Lorelei had drowned, and a short, unsigned note. It said, and I quote exactly, "You are responsible for this. You gave her foolish dreams." I guess . . .' Terrill's voice grew husky '. . . he was trying to tell me that she drowned herself. I was depressed for a long time after that, and swore I'd never let myself get close to anyone again. And I didn't, until I met you.'

Tears were streaming down Claire's cheeks. 'Oh, Terrill,' she said, stroking his cheek with a trembling hand, 'I'm so sorry. I should have . . .'

'Oh, there you are!' Jayne's cheerful voice interrupted. 'Mr Forsythe's been trying to reach you two. He says come on over to the hotel. To do with something being fishy at his meeting with someone.'

Terrill pushed himself to a sitting position.

'Now what?' he muttered. He looked down at Claire and sighed. 'I guess we'd better go and find out.'

Claire nodded, mopping at her tears with her beach towel. She felt wrung out from the strain of her secret knowledge. She got to her feet and gathered up her things. What should she do?

'Come on,' Terrill said impatiently, obviously unhappy at having their talk interrupted.

'I'm coming,' Claire replied. She would have to wait just a little longer.

Roger Forsythe was quite agitated when they met him in the drawing-room of the Forsythes' suite.

'The man was perfectly civil,' he said, 'but several things he said simply didn't add up. He told me that he had to let Harold Hanover go because he drank.

Harold never touched liquor. He said that he had dispersed his herd of cattle. If he had, I'd have heard about it from some of the other ranches. No one can sell that many cattle without word getting around. And . . .' he looked at Terrill and smiled wryly ' . . . contrary to what you told me, he said you were a very fine man. A credit to your country, he said.'

Terrill shrugged. 'Maybe time has softened his attitude towards me.'

'N—no!' Claire interrupted. 'It hasn't. When I had to see him about his wandering cattle, he called you evil and a devil. I never saw anyone express such hatred for another person.'

'Why didn't you tell me that?' Terrill demanded, scowling.

'Because I thought he was crazy,' Claire replied. 'I couldn't see any point in burdening you with such nonsense.'

'Well, I wish you'd told me,' Terrill repeated, giving Claire another dark frown before he turned to Roger Forsythe. 'Shall we go and have that look around, after all?'

'I think we should,' Roger Forsythe agreed. 'Let's go in by your property. I want to scout around for some signs of how recently cattle have been there.'

'I'm coming with you,' Claire said.

Her father gave her a forbidding look. 'No, my dear, you are not. You stay and keep your mother company. She'll get worried if she's left alone.'

'B—but . . .' Claire's heart sank. She could yell at Terrill and get her own way, but it would not work with her father. She felt sick and trembling, the sense of foreboding closing in on her now like a dense cloud. What if Ben Williams saw Terrill coming? What might he do to him? What might he do to his poor daughter?

'Terrill, wait!' she called out, as the two men started for the door. 'There's something else I haven't told you.'

'What is it?' Terrill asked. 'Can't it keep until we get back?'

'No!' Claire cried, her voice a harsh-sounding rasp in her own ears above the pounding of her heart. 'Lorelei isn't dead! Jayne and I saw her.'

'You what?' Terrill wheeled round to face Claire. He put his hands on her shoulders and shook her, his face a terrible combination of rage and disbelief. 'Why are you telling me this lie?' he demanded.

'It's not a lie,' Claire gasped out between chattering teeth. 'You know the night after Jayne came, when I was late getting back to the villa? We'd gone to the beach to watch for the ghost, and . . .'

'You idiot!' Terrill interrupted at a roar. 'What kind of ridiculous nonsense are you throwing in my face? I loved that woman. She drowned herself because of me! Don't you think I've suffered enough? I don't need lies about her ghost haunting the beach where we made love!'

'She's not a ghost, she's alive!' Claire screamed. 'Believe me, she's as alive as you and me! She didn't drown. Ben Williams is the one who lied!'

'Then why in God's name didn't you tell me?' Terrill rasped, flinging Claire away from him so abruptly that she staggered back and fell into a chair. 'Never mind. I don't give a damn. I've got to get to her before . . .' He turned back to Roger Forsythe, who was taking in the scene with a look of disbelief. 'Let's go. We're going to have to figure out how to approach this so that maniac doesn't do anything foolish.'

'Don't you think . . . you ought to take the police with you?' Mrs Forsythe said, as the door closed behind the two men. She turned to Claire, who was doubled over in her chair, sobbing bitterly. 'Oh, dear, first your father and now you. What's the matter, baby? Did Mr Hawkes upset you, yelling at you like that? I'm sure he'll be all right, once they find that girl.'

Claire shook her head. 'No, Mother, he won't,' she sobbed. 'He won't ever forgive me, if something happens to her, and if she's all right . . .' she looked at her mother with tragic eyes '. . . if she's all right, it won't matter. I love him, and he loves her.'

Mrs Forsythe sighed. 'I thought you did, as soon as I saw you two together.' She carried a box of tissues to Claire. 'Dry your tears, dear, then come and sit beside me on the sofa and tell me all about it.' When Claire, still tearful, had curled up next to her, she asked, 'Is that why you didn't tell him about the girl?'

'I guess so,' Claire replied. 'Of course, at first I didn't know about him and Lorelei. He never told me, until today. I just put things together, a little at a time, and figured it out.' She leaned her head on her mother's shoulder. 'There's a lot I didn't get to tell him,' she said. 'Maybe it's just as well.'

'Tell me,' her mother said, patting Claire's head as if she were a child. 'It will help to talk about it.'

Haltingly, Claire told her mother the details of that evening when she and Jayne had seen the ghostly little dancer, then the story that Terrill had told her only that afternoon.

'You know, dear,' Mrs Forsythe said thoughtfully, 'I'm afraid you may be right that Lorelei is unbalanced. I studied psychology in college, you know, when I was working towards my teaching credentials. It sounds to me as if the poor girl has been seriously disturbed for a long time, even when Terrill first knew her. That may be why her father kept her confined. It's all so very sad, isn't it? Your Terrill may have loved someone who could never have brought him happiness, after all. I wonder what he will do, if your suspicions are right?'

Claire shook her head, tears running down her cheeks once again. 'I don't know. I only wish . . .' She buried her face in her mother's shoulder. 'I wish he loved me,' she sobbed.

'I think you're being very premature in deciding he doesn't,' her mother scolded gently. 'He's a big man. There may be room in his heart for both of you. Now, let's send down for some tea and something light to eat while we wait. I never even had a proper lunch today.'

It was after dark when Roger Forsythe returned, alone, Claire had got her emotions under control, but one look at her father's face and she felt tears close again.

'What happened?' she demanded, almost in chorus with her mother.

Roger Forsythe shook his head, poured himself a drink, and then sat down. 'Williams is in police custody. We did get them to go with us, and he offered no resistance at all. I think things had finally gotten so far out of hand that the didn't know what to do next. Apparently he finally succeeded in bringing in some cattle without proper inspection. He also brought in foot and mouth disease, which, as you know, is one of the most lethal and virulent diseases of cattle. To his credit, he destroyed his whole herd and buried them in an immense trench he made with a bulldozer. Harold Hanover had insisted he must tell the authorities. To silence him, William locked him up in a small shed on the property, then made it look as if he'd moved away from his home. The poor fellow's had nothing to eat for over a week, but again, to Williams' credit, he did give him water.'

'But he would have starved!' Mrs Forsythe cried.

'Williams claimed he planned to let him out soon,' her husband replied, 'although I don't believe him after seeing what he did to that poor daughter of his.'

Claire could stand it no longer. She leaned forward in her chair. 'What about Lorelei? What about Terrill? What happened when they met?'

Again, Roger Forsythe shook his head, looking infinitely sad. 'Lorelei was locked in her bedroom, a place so filthy you wouldn't believe it. She herself was relatively clean, but she was wearing only some kind of a shift. When she saw Terrill, she recognised him immediately. He held out his arms to her and she ran to him.' He paused, took a long draught of his drink, then gave Claire and her mother a meaningful look. 'Terrill said something like, "My poor Lorelei." She said, "Terrill, where were you last night? I missed you." I've never seen a man look as shattered as he did at that moment.'

'Oh, no!' Claire said, her heart aching in sympathy for what Terrill must have felt. Would it have been any easier for him if she had told him what she had seen? She would never know. 'Poor Terrill. What . . . what is he going to do now?'

'He's taken the girl . . . I suppose she's really a woman, but she's so small and thin she looks younger . . . He's taken her to the local hospital for the night. As soon as she's been checked over, he'll be taking her back to the States for treatment. Probably tomorrow, he said. I doubt the prognosis is very good, but I know he'll do all he can to help her. He feels guilty that he wasn't more persistent in the first place in getting her away from her father.'

'I'm sure he will,' Claire said softly. Terrill would probably devote his life to trying to make up for something that wasn't his fault at all. She looked from her father to her mother. 'Do you mind if I stay here tonight? I don't want to go back to the villa.' Terrill would be going back there to pack, and she couldn't bear to face him. She wasn't sure she would ever be able to face him again.

CHAPTER ELEVEN

IT SEEMED very strange to be holding the grand opening of the Jamaican Star without Terrill Hawkes. In his stead he had sent Payton Woodbine, his austere-looking vice president, with his socialite wife at his side. The Woodbines made an adequately elegant impression on the glittering array of guests who had arrived for the holiday affair. Ernest, dapper in a dinner-jacket, was circulating serenely among the crowd, greeting them all with his easy charm. Claire was glad that Terrill had agreed to her suggestion that he be made assistant manager. Ernest was easily the best goodwill ambassador that Jamaica could have. His help had been invaluable since Terrill Hawkes had left with Lorelei, never to return. Without him, Claire knew, she could not have got the hotel ready to open in time for the Christmas-New Year holidays.

In spite of her busy schedule, the days had dragged by for Claire. After Terrill had gone, she had written him a long letter, apologising for not telling him sooner about seeing Lorelei, and offering her best wishes and prayers that Lorelei would get well. In return she received a stiff little note, telling her that she was not to feel guilty about her omission, and that doctors did hold out some hope that new drug therapies might help Lorelei. There was even a chance that she might one day be able to fulfil her long-held dream of studying dance. His own plans were to stay in the States and see that Lorelei had the best possible treatment. She seemed so dependent on his presence that he did not want to let her down again. Claire, he knew, would understand, and he had complete confidence in her ability to finish the job on the hotel.

Claire shed bitter tears over the letter, more from its completely unemotional tone than from what it said. It was as if nothing at all had happened between them. Perhaps it hadn't, she told herself sadly. Perhaps she had only imagined that he had said he felt close to her, and that his kisses had been so passionate that she'd been sure he loved her. Or it could be that, now he had Lorelei back, no matter what her condition, he realised that his love for Lorelei completely overshadowed what he had felt for Claire, and was embarrassed at the overtures he had made.

Whatever the case, Claire realised that she might never know. She pulled herself together, resolved to forget as quickly as possible. When Terrill called, which he did several times, to find out how the hotel was progressing, she was brisk and businesslike, in spite of the fact that the sound of his voice turned her insides to jelly. If talking to her gave Terrill any qualms, it was not apparent in his voice. He even told her, quite calmly, one day in early December that Lorelei was now well enough for him to take her to New York by Christmas time and enrol her in a dancing class.

'I'm very glad to hear that,' Claire replied, and she truly was. She still loved Terrill with all her heart, and she knew that having his beloved Lorelei doing so well must make him very happy. 'I'll be going home for Christmas,' she added, 'as soon as the hotel opens. I never did get that vacation you promised me.'

'Of course,' Terrill readily agreed. 'You deserve it. Take a couple of months off. I have nothing planned right now.'

And so it was with very mixed emotions that Claire watched the island of Jamaica disappear from view as the plane headed north. So much had happened there. She would never be the same. She would always love Terrill Hawkes. She would always remember the first time she saw him there, so different from the man she had known before, but still, really, the same, the only change being that the vulnerable man beneath the bluster had come to the fore. The villa, Terrill's Paradise, was different now, too. The redecoration completed, it was lovely and light and airy-looking, filled with bright colours and comfortable furnishings. Claire wondered if Terrill would ever bring Lorelei there, or whether she would want to stay far from the beautiful land where her life had been so sadly confined by her father. That pitiful man was still in custody, facing charges going back to the questionable death of his wife, but too unstable to stand trial.

The Jamaican Star was as brilliant as Terrill had hoped, destined to pamper the most discriminating traveller in luxurious surroundings for many years to come. It was now a fitting addition to the land of brilliant sunshine, gorgeous colours, and handsome, friendly people, from which it took its name.

'What's wrong, Claire?' Jayne asked, as Claire heaved a sigh and then leaned her head back against the seat cushion and closed her eyes.

'Nothing. And everything,' Claire replied, opening her eyes and giving Jayne a sad little smile. 'I feel as if I'm leaving part of me behind.'

Jayne reached over and squeezed Claire's hand in sympathy. 'Me, too.' She had dithered for days over whether to stay in Jamaica. Jim Raines had seemed on the verge of proposing, but when he did not by the time the hotel opening drew near, Jayne decided that her absence might be more apt to get him off the mark than having her stay around, obviously waiting.

'I think it's a good thing we have each other's company,' Claire said. 'I'd hate to be making this trip alone.'

'Misery loves company,' Jayne replied, nodding in agreement.

At Miami, the two women boarded a plane for Chicago. Jayne lived near that midwestern city, and Claire's mother was scheduled to meet her there and stay on for a couple of days of Christmas shopping before they returned home.

'You look like a brown toothpick,' was Mrs Forsythe's first remark upon seeing her daughter. 'Haven't you been eating anything?'

'I've been too busy,' Claire replied. 'You can fatten me up as soon as we get home. My, isn't it nice to have some snow for Christmas?' she added, trying to change the topic which she was afraid her mother would pursue at length.

'I'd as soon have some of that Jamaican sunshine,' Mrs Forsythe replied. 'It's been nasty and cold since November.' She looked at her daughter critically. 'I think you've been pining. What you need is to get back with your family that loves you. I think it was unforgivable of Mr Hawkes to run off and leave you with all of that work to do alone. A man who would do that isn't worthy of you.'

'He had his reasons,' Claire said tightly. 'You know that. I don't want to talk about it. All I want to do now is find some nice presents for everyone and then go home and forget all about Mr Hawkes and Jamaica.

The more it snows, the better I'll like it.'

Mrs Forsythe sighed but said nothing. She knew her daughter, and there was unlikely to be enough snow in all of North America to erase her longing for that man. How long, she wondered, would it be before Claire's eyes would sparkle as they used to? It was hard for a mother to see her daughter so unhappy and know there was nothing she could do to help except watch and wait for time to pass.

The Christmas season did help to distract Claire, as did her three-year-old nephew and a baby niece she had not seen before. There were parties with old friends, and a New Year's celebration at the Forsythe house to which Harold Hanover came. He had decided to return to the University of Illinois and pursue an advanced degree. But after the holidays Claire's spirits took a downturn. There was no word from Terrill Hawkes on any new projects, and the only word at Christmas had been a large poinsettia plant addressed to the whole Forsythe family, which Claire was sure some secretary had been told to send.

'For all I know, I may be out of a job,' she complained when her father commented that her smile had faded along with her tan.

'Are you sure you still want to work for Hawkes?' her father asked.

'No, I'm not,' she replied. 'I'm not sure of that at all.'

The more she had thought about it, the more she had thought her mother was right. Lorelei or no Lorelei, Terrill Hawkes had treated her very shabbily. He was not so dense that he hadn't been aware that she cared very deeply for him. To leave her swinging in the wind, with no word at all about their personal relationship for so long, was unforgivable. Did he think he could put her on hold like a telephone call for ever? Or did he think, after what he had told her about his love for Lorelei, that she would understand that she had been merely an interim dalliance, and he needn't bother with any explanations? That would certainly be true to form. He hadn't been exactly forthcoming with explanations about his strange behaviour when he got to Jamaica.

Now, it seemed, there wasn't even anything about Hawkes Hotels that he wanted to communicate with her about. Well, if he didn't get in touch with her pretty soon, she was going to quit and look for work elsewhere. When the month of January ended and February began with still no word, she grimly faced the fact that Terrill Hawkes apparently wanted nothing more to do with her.

'I'm sending in my resignation to Mr Hawkes,' she announced to her parents one morning at breakfast. 'Don't try to stop me. I've got a résumé almost ready to start sending around to prospective employers.'

'I won't try to stop you, dear,' her mother said with a sigh, 'but are you quite sure that resigning is the answer? You did like your work so much.'

'In case you haven't noticed,' Claire said wryly, 'I haven't been working lately.' She looked at her father, who raised his eyebrows and shrugged.

'I can't say that I blame you,' he said, 'but are you sure it's your head that made the decision, and not your heart?'

'Some of both,' Claire replied, lifting her chin defiantly. 'I do have both of them with me at all times.'

After her letter was posted, Claire tried valiantly not to let her mind focus on what response she might get from Terrill Hawkes, but it insisted on speculating, no matter how hard she tried to think of other things.

Would he be glad? Sorry? Would she even be able to tell which he was from the letter he would write? Somehow, it did not occur to her that he might call. When, only three days after her letter was mailed, her mother told her that Mr Hawkes was on the telephone for her, she was not even sure that he would have received her letter. His first words told her that he had.

'Miss Forsythe,' he shouted, his voice almost loud enough to have been heard for two thousand miles without the use of telephone lines, 'what is this ridiculous piece of paper I have before me?'

The sound of that familiar roar set both Claire's eardrum and nerves to vibrating. Did that idiot think he could now pick up where they had left off almost a year ago? Go back to being 'Mr Hawkes' and 'Miss Forsythe' as if nothing at all had happened in between?

'How should I know?' she snapped back. 'I can't see through the telephone.' But how she wished they both could, so that he could see how absolutely furious she was!

'It says,' came a reply in loudly scathing tones, "Dear Mr Hawkes, I hereby resign my position with Hawkes Hotels. Thank you for everything. I trust I can count on you for a good recommendation as I seek employment elsewhere." What do you mean, you resign?'

'I mean exactly that! I quit!' Claire replied. 'Isn't it clear enough for you?'

'Why?' Terrill Hawkes demanded. 'Why are you resigning?'

'Because I don't want to work for you any more,' Claire answered, her stomach in a miserable knot as she said so. She could picture him so clearly now. Having to see him, day after day, and know that he could never be hers would be unbearable. No matter what his shortcomings, she still loved him. That, however, was the last reason on earth that she would give him. 'I've decided I want a job with less responsibility and more regular hours,' she added, keeping her voice icily calm. 'I have no intention of sacrificing myself on the altar of Hawkes Hotels, especially since you seem to take so little interest in them any more.'

There was the muffled sound of cursing on Terrill Hawkes' end of the line. 'That is grossly unfair, Miss Forsythe, and you know it! However, I have no intention of discussing that topic with you over the telephone. The least I expect is for you to do me the courtesy of coming to New York to present your grievances and give me a chance to reply. I refuse to accept your resignation until you do.'

'You refuse?' Claire's voice rose in indignation. 'What do you think I am, your slave? Don't answer that. You obviously do. Well, let me tell you, Mr Hawkes, that I am not. Nor am I about to come to New York to listen to your excuses. You haven't really communicated with me in almost a year, and now you expect good old Miss Forsythe to snap to and say "yes, sir!" when you call. Well, let me tell you, *Mr* Hawkes, it makes absolutely no difference to me whether you accept my resignation or not! I quit!'

'*Miss* Forsythe, I will expect you here on Monday morning,' came the stubborn reply.

'*Mr* Hawkes, you can expect from now until kingdom come, but I will not be there,' came the equally stubborn answer. 'If you are so dead set on talking to me in person, you can come here to do it. Goodbye!' With that, Claire slammed down the receiver with such force that her father, who had come into the room to see what all the shouting was about, winced.

'Careful,' he said. 'They don't make telephones like they used to. What was that all about?'

'That was about the most impossible man who ever lived!' Claire cried, still loudly upset. 'He says he won't accept my resignation.'

'You would be hard to replace,' her father said reasonably. 'Not many people could do all of the things that my Claire does so well.'

'Thank you, Daddy,' Claire said, making a face and trying to calm her seething temper. 'But you know as well as I do that no one is irreplaceable. I'm sure Mr Hawkes will realise it too, as soon as he's gotten over the shock. I wouldn't expect him to come out here to beg me to stay on. Especially if it means leaving his dear Lorelei.'

Roger Forsythe frowned at his daughter. 'You sound as though you resent his attentions to that poor girl.'

'Well, I do,' Claire replied. 'I know I shouldn't, but I do, and it makes me feel guilty. I want her to get better and to be able to dance, but the last thing on earth I want is for her to marry Terrill Hawkes and live happily ever after.'

'You don't know that he's planning to marry her, do you?' her father asked.

'Good heavens, what else would he be planning to do? He's been with her for almost a year! Do you realise that I haven't even seen the man since last March?' Claire's voice rose again in agitation. 'Why on earth should he be surprised that I decided to resign? It's like working for a ghost! If he does come here, I'm not even going to talk to him. Enough is enough!'

'Now, dear,' her mother said, 'that wouldn't be

polite.'

'Polite!' Claire wailed. 'Good lord, Mother, why should I worry about being polite? When we were in Jamaica, he called me Claire, and I thought for a while, I really did, that he loved me! And now he's back to calling me Miss Forsythe again!' With that, she burst into tears and hurried from the room.

CHAPTER TWELVE

CLAIRE ran up the stairs, sobbing, and flung herself on her bed, clutching her old teddy bear which had lain there since she'd got him out for her baby niece to play with. It was all over now. If she had held out some shred of hope before, it was gone, dashed for ever by Terrill's 'Miss Forsythe'. He was obviously trying to tell her that it was back to business as usual as far as he was concerned. Well, this time it wasn't. Nothing Terrill Hawkes could say or do would convince her to continue working for him.

'Claire, dear?' Mrs Forsythe tapped on the door and then poked her head into the room.

'Come in, Mother,' Claire said, reaching for a tissue and blowing her nose vigorously. 'I'm all right,' she said, as her mother came to her side, an anxious frown puckering her forehead.

'I know,' her mother replied. She looked down at Claire's teddy bear and smiled. 'Good old Bear. He's been around a long time, hasn't he?'

Claire nodded. 'He's soaked up a lot of tears over the years. No wonder his coat is so matted down.' She fingered the bear's button nose. 'I guess if he could talk, he'd remind me that life goes on, wouldn't he?'

'I expect he would,' her mother agreed. 'You know, dear, I did want to tell you one thing I remembered just now. It might explain why Mr Hawkes has gone back to calling you Miss Forsythe again.'

'What's that?' Claire asked.

'Well, you know when your father and I met, I was already a schoolteacher. At first, for quite a while, he very respectfully called me Miss Martin, just as my first graders did. At least, I thought he was being respectful. Then I found out that he called other women by their first names, so I asked him to call me Louise and he did. Later he explained that he fell in love with me right away, and wasn't sure how I felt, so that calling me Miss Martin made him feel safer. Louise seemed too . . . too intimate.'

'Somehow, I don't think that's Terrill's problem,' Claire said with a sigh.

'Maybe not,' said Mrs Forsythe, 'but every time your father and I had a fight, he'd go back to calling me Miss Martin. Retreating to safer ground, he said, when I asked him about it. Of course, all it did was make me wonder what I'd done wrong, so it wasn't very helpful. But then, men aren't always very smart about such things. They have their own way of looking at the world, and it doesn't always make much sense.'

'I'll certainly agree with that,' Claire said with feeling. 'And if it weren't for Lorelei, I might think you're right.' She shook her head. 'I do wish I knew what has been happening to her. If she were the traditional other woman, I'd at least be able to fight it, but the way things are . . .'

'I know, dear,' Mrs Forsythe said, giving Claire a hug. 'You're being very brave. I do think, though, that you should give Mr Hawkes a chance to have his say when he comes.'

'*If* he comes,' Claire said, 'I shall try to be polite. Meanwhile, I don't want to think about him at all. Isn't there a sale somewhere that we could go to?'

'Why, yes!' Mrs Forsythe's eyes brightened at the prospect of a shopping expedition. 'Winter coats are

on sale now, and you could use a new one. We could
have lunch and then shop the afternoon away.'

'That sounds great,' Claire said, grimly determined
to be distracted. 'Give me a few minutes to get ready,
and we'll go.'

It was after dark, and huge snowflakes were drifting
lazily down when Claire and her mother returned
home to the big, square brick house on the edge of
town.

'I do wish your father and I didn't have that date for
dinner and bridge tonight,' Mrs Forsythe said as they
got out of the car with their armloads of packages. 'I
don't like to leave you alone tonight.'

'I'll be fine, Mother,' Claire assured her. 'I'll just
have some pizza and watch TV. I feel a lot better now,
really.' She led the way up the stairs to the wide front
porch, stamping her feet to remove the sticky snow,
then opened the door and stepped inside. She set her
packages on the staircase, then turned to remove her
coat. Suddenly, she became aware of male voices in
the living-room, which opened off the central hallway.

'Oh, my God!' she exclaimed, freezing in position
with her coat in one hand. One of the voices was her
father's. The other was, unmistakably, Terrill
Hawkes!

'What is it, dear?' her mother asked, seeing Claire's
ashen face. 'Are you ill?'

'It—it's him!' she whispered. 'Terrill Hawkes. In
there!' She gestured towards the living-room. 'What
shall I do?'

'Keep your chin up and go and say hello,' her
mother replied firmly. 'Here, give me that coat.' She
flung both of their coats across a chair, then took
Claire's arm. 'Come along,' she said to her still immo-

bile daughter.

Claire felt her feet moving beneath her as if they belonged to some other person. Her brain had ceased to function at all. There was a faint buzzing sound in her ears, as if all of her mental gears had started to slip, freewheeling but producing nothing. Her heart pounded so hard that it made her whole body shake in its rhythm.

'Ah, there the shoppers are now,' her father said, and for a moment Claire had no idea where his words came from. The whole room seemed filled by Terrill Hawkes, taller, thinner, and immeasurably more handsome than she had remembered. His dark hair had noticeable splashes of grey at the temples now, and the heavy black turtleneck sweater he wore accented a face more deeply lined, more pale, than she had ever seen it. The bright blue of his eyes was still there, so intense that it seemed to light the space between them. The eyes shifted away from hers, and Claire watched as he greeted her mother.

'Hello, Mrs Forsythe,' Terrill said, inclining his head graciously and extending his hand.

Claire felt her mother's hand leave her arm as she took Terrill's hand and shook it.

'Hello, Mr Hawkes. What a pleasant surprise.'

'Thank you,' Terrill replied. He turned towards Claire and very slowly held his hand out towards her. 'Hello . . . Claire.'

Claire! He had called her Claire! His face shimmered through a sudden mist. Somehow, her hand found its way into that huge hand, her brain registering in surprise that it felt almost as cold and clammy as her own.

'H—hello,' she said, her voice sounding like an echo in her own ears.

'Mother, I think we'd better be going,' she heard her father say. 'Isn't there some place still open where we can buy you a mink coat?'

That bizarre statement made Claire jerk her head around to look at her parents at the same time as her mother let out a little gasp.

'Roger Forsythe,' she said, 'we can't afford . . .'

'Oh, I think we can,' Mr Forsythe said, taking his wife's arm and leading her towards the doorway. 'I think I just won one in a lottery.'

'You did what?' his wife cried, her voice squeaking in astonishment.

Roger Forsythe turned back and winked at Terrill Hawkes. 'We won't be back until late,' he said. A few moments later, the outside door closed behind them, leaving Claire standing, her hand still in Terrill's grasp, and her mind more befuddled than ever. Had her father really won a mink coat for her mother? Or was that just some ruse that he and Terrill had cooked up to leave the two of them alone? If so, she wasn't sure she appreciated it. Or . . . her eyes returned to Terrill's face. Or did she?

'Wh—what's going on?' she demanded, trying unsuccessfully to pull her hand free.

'You mean the mink coat?' Terrill asked. When Claire nodded, he replied, 'It's just a little wager that your father and I had. He seems to think he's won.' He cocked his head and looked thoughtfully at Claire. 'I'm not so sure, myself.'

'Oh.' Claire's mind was beginning to function now. Apparently, Terrill had been here for some time, discussing things with her father, who must have bet that she was not going to stick to her decision to resign. They must have been very large odds, too, for her father never bet more than nickels and dimes! Claire frowned. 'I suppose he bet that I wouldn't resign, after all,' she said.

Terrill shook his head. 'No, that's not it at all. In fact, I don't really care whether you do or not.' He smiled, that shy little smile Claire had seen when he first arrived in Jamaica. 'Whatever you want to do will be all right with me. First, though, we have a lot to talk about. I have a lot to tell you. Let's sit down, shall we?'

'All right,' Claire replied, letting Terrill lead her to the large leather sofa which sat before the fireplace in the Forsythes' comfortable living-room. He was certainly right in that he had a lot of explaining to do! But if he no longer cared whether she resigned, why was he here? She sat down in one corner of the sofa, watching Terrill's face closely for some clue as he carefully settled himself in the middle. He turned sideways to face her, one elbow on the back of the sofa. For what seemed to Claire like an eternity he studied her, still with that tentative little smile. Finally, he took a deep breath.

'I guess the first thing I need to do,' Terrill said, his face very serious again, 'is to tell you about Lorelei.'

At the sound of those words, Claire's heart almost stopped. Was that what he was here for, after all this time? To plunge the knife in, in person? She wanted to scream out, 'No! Don't tell me!' but something deep and sad in Terrill's eyes stilled her. She nodded almost imperceptibly, wondering if her heart would ever beat again after she heard what he was about to say.

'She is now living with a ballet master and his wife,' Terrill went on. 'They are very warm, kind people. Over the years, they've taken in a number of troubled young dancers. There are two other, younger girls living there now. Having them to talk to gives Lorelei a chance to go back and catch up on some of the life she missed.'

'That's . . . that's very nice,' Claire said, as Terrill paused, seeming to have difficulty with his next words. But what did that mean? That Lorelei and Terrill . . .

As if reading her unspoken question, Terrill nodded. 'Yes, it is,' he said, 'but I expect you're wondering about Lorelei and me?' He looked at Claire, raising his eyebrows questioningly.

'I . . . yes,' Claire replied faintly.

Terrill cleared his throat and looked down at his hands. 'Lorelei understands now,' he said, 'that I am her friend, and will always be there for her when she needs me. I, in turn, understand a great many things about Lorelei and my feelings towards her that I didn't before. I'll tell you more about that later.' He looked back at Claire, the lines of tension deep about his eyes. 'What I really came here to talk about is you and me,' he said softly, his eyes searching Claire's face intensely. 'I hope there's still something to talk about, after this past year.'

A rush of warmth flooded Claire's heart, seeming to set her entire body on fire with an explosion of hope. Did Terrill mean what she thought he meant? She opened her mouth to speak, but no words would come. She shook her head, trying to clear her mind. Terrill's face fell. Good lord, he thought she meant no!

'Terrill, I didn't mean . . .' she began. Then, as if her bursting heart could stand it no longer, she flung herself into his arms, burying her face against his neck and sobbing.

'Oh, Claire,' Terrill said, his voice husky, 'I'm sorry.' He patted her back comfortingly. 'I was afraid it had been too long. It's not your fault. I shouldn't have expected . . . don't feel sad, please. Is it someone else?'

'Someone else?' Claire choked out between sobs. She drew her head back and looked into his dear, sweet face. 'You idiot!' she cried. 'I love you, Terrill Hawkes, I love *you!*'

Terrill stared at her, at first in disbelief. Then, as if dawn had come bursting into the room, he smiled, that wonderful, happy smile that Claire adored. His arms grasped her, first tentatively, and then with crushing strength. She could feel the pounding of his heart, hear him breathing hard, as if he were trying to control some violent emotion. Suddenly he held her a little away from him, his eyes so bright with love that she was almost blinded by their light.

'Say that again,' he whispered, his own lashes sparkling with tears of happiness.

'I love you,' she answered, first softly and then in a joyous cry as he now smiled as if all of the sunshine in the world had been gathered inside of him.

'Oh, Claire,' he said, 'I love you, I adore you. I always have and I always will.' He pulled her close again, his mouth closing over hers with such passion that every thought again fled from her mind, leaving her giddy with surges of elation that seemed to transport her into another world. His hands explored her body with urgent eagerness, pushing inside her sweater to touch her bare skin. She tugged at his sweater, longing to feel the warmth of his body, the strength that was at once so powerful and so gentle.

'Whoa, there! Wait a minute,' he said, pulling his

head back as she at last succeeded. He smiled that dazzling smile again. 'Would you like to keep that promise now?' he asked.

Claire laughed. 'You bet I would,' she replied. 'I think it's long overdue. Shall I show you the way to my room?'

'In a minute,' Terrill replied. 'Maybe. But first, you may recall that I said on a certain day that I planned to extract a different promise from you, and I'm afraid we can go no further until I do.'

'Now what?' Claire asked impatiently.

Terrill smiled mischievously as Claire pouted. 'I also told you I thought I knew the right man for you to marry. Here I am, Claire Forsythe. Will you marry me?' Terrill laughed as Claire's eyes grew huge, her mouth opened, and she again found no sound would emerge. 'Is that a yes?' he asked. 'It had better be, because I won't take no for an answer.'

'Yes, yes, yes!' she shouted, finding her voice at last.

'Right answer!' Terrill said triumphantly, scooping Claire into his arms and kissing her. 'Your father was right. It's a good thing he encouraged me,' he added as Claire frowned, 'or I might not have had the courage to ask. And now, would the very-soon-to-be Mrs Terrill Hawkes tell me the way to her bedroom?'

Flying up the stairs in Terrill's arms, Claire thought how utterly mad she would have believed anyone who told her this would be happening to her on this day. Together, they merged their naked bodies beneath the soft covers on Claire's big, comfortable four-poster bed, straining to stay close, to touch every delicious spot that now belonged to them as one. At first, Terrill only held Claire close, his eyes devouring her face, his hands caressing her silky skin, his lips murmuring words of love between kisses that drove her desire to heights she had never dreamed possible. When, at last, he possessed her and the waves of release came crashing through her, she felt tears of joy overflowing and saw that Terrill was sharing the same feelings.

'My dearest little one, my treasure,' he murmured, his lips nuzzling her ear. 'Why didn't you tell me you hadn't been with a man before?'

'Because I didn't want you to worry about hurting me,' Claire replied, stroking the dark hair, so thick and silky, back from Terrill's forehead. 'I didn't think it would hurt, and it didn't.'

Terrill sighed. 'You were so eager, back there in Jamaica, that I assumed you had. I've been wrong about so many things. Why didn't I just ask you to marry me that day in Las Vegas instead of putting you off with some nonsense about not wanting anything but sex from a woman?'

'I don't know,' Claire said softly, 'why didn't you? I'd probably have said yes.'

'Because, at the time, I really believed that was all I wanted,' Terrill replied. He shifted so that Claire's head was on his shoulder, and smiled down at her. 'I had no insight into the reason I felt that way. Oh, I knew that my experience with Lorelei had been a bitter, unhappy one, but I thought I had made a perfectly sane, objective decision to keep my distance from women so that it wouldn't happen again. I had no idea, until I fell in love with you, how deeply it had scarred me, and how terrified I was that another love might be snatched from me just as I thought she had been.'

'My poor darling,' Claire said, caressing his cheek tenderly. 'I wish I had known. I might have been able to help.'

Terrill shook his head. 'I don't think anyone could have, at least, not until I realised I had a problem. Then, once I did, day by day I fought it, trying to understand. At last I realised what must be wrong, and decided that I must go back to Jamaica and face the demons that were haunting me. I needed to go to the places where I'd been with Lorelei, and I wanted to face her father once more and hear from him the story of her death. Perhaps, somehow, I never really believed she'd drowned herself. I also realised that it was time to stop pretending that I thought of you merely as a business associate. I wanted so desperately to be close to you, to find out if you could love me as I loved you. I thought that if we could only be together in Jamaica I could accomplish both things. It turned out to be a lot more difficult than I'd thought.' He paused and smiled his brilliant, loving smile. 'I wish you could have seen your face the first time I called you Claire. You looked absolutely appalled.'

'And I wish you could have seen mine yesterday, when you went back to calling me Miss Forsythe,' Claire replied, wrinkling her nose at him. 'I hadn't really given up all hope that you cared for me until then, and it made me so unhappy and angry at the same time . . . I didn't know what to do.'

'I'm sorry, my love,' Terrill said softly, his expression clouded. 'I don't ever want to make you unhappy again. The reason I did that was because I was equally afraid that all of my hopes had been dashed. The letter you wrote me after I left Jamaica sounded so much like a goodbye, and when I talked with you, you sounded so very businesslike again, that I was worried all along. But until I got your resignation, I hadn't really given up all hope, either.'

'Why didn't you come to see me?' Claire asked. 'Surely you could have told me something, asked me something, that would have cleared things up. I thought you didn't care, after all, once you'd found Lorelei again.'

Terrill sighed heavily, the lines about his eyes drawing in in pain. 'I wasn't sure, at first, if that might not be true. The shock was so great, finding Lorelei like that. I thought I might be to blame for everything that was wrong with her. It took some time for me to accept the fact that she had been just as ill when I first knew her. At that time, I thought her strange moods were all because of her father, and that she would be fine if she were away from him. I was very young and naïve, and hadn't had any experience with someone who was mentally ill like that. The doctors helped me as much as they've helped her, I think.'

'What do you mean?'

'They reassured me, educated me, taught me how to deal with Lorelei without being trapped in an endless chain of alternately feeling guilt and blaming others as her father had done, trying to do more than anyone can do in such cases. They also assured me that it would be best to lead my own life, with you, as I'd wanted to all along.'

'And then you got my resignation.' Claire said sadly. 'I'm so sorry. If I'd only known. But then, I guess you hadn't really given up, after all. You are here now, aren't you? Or am I dreaming? I still can't quite believe this is happening.'

'Believe it,' Terrill said, flashing a smile and giving Claire a little pinch. 'No, I guess deep down I hadn't given up. Maybe I never would have. I have been known to be persistent, you know.'

'You mean stubborn?' Claire teased. She laughed as Terrill nipped at her neck, then crushed her against him, moving his body so that he could begin to explore hers with his hands once again. 'Mmmm,' Claire breathed, beginning explorations of her own. 'I do believe there's something you want more of.'

Terrill groaned and smiled sleepily. 'How right you are. But before we begin again, can I tell you one more thing about Lorelei? I want to be absolutely sure you understand how I feel about her.'

'I know you still love her,' Claire said, touching Terrill's lips softly with her own. 'I wouldn't want to change that. She needs to know it, too.'

'Yes,' Terrill said. 'She does. But the love I have for her now is much more like a brother or father, and she understands that. The funny thing is . . .' he smiled wryly '. . . that her first love always was and is her dancing. Even if things had been very different, I would always have been second fiddle to that.'

'I can understand that,' Claire said. She smiled mischievously. 'My first love will always be Hawkes Hotels.'

Terrill put on a dark frown.

'Miss Forsythe,' he roared softly, 'you are fired!'

'No, I'm not,' she replied airily. 'I quit. I can no longer work for you, Mr Hawkes, I have a family to raise.'

'Your resignation is accepted, at least temporarily,' Terrill replied, kissing Claire's lips tenderly. 'But when the children are all in school . . .' He paused. 'How many did you have in mind?'

'I don't know.' Claire shook her head. It still felt unreal, being asked that question, here in Terrill's arms. 'I never even let myself think about that. Two, three, four? And let's spend a lot of time with them at the villa. It's so cosy and pretty now.'

'We will. I'm anxious to see it. We can spend our honeymoon there, if you like. And we'll find a place in the country here, too, with room for ponies for the children, and dogs. Golden retrievers, wasn't it, we decided on?'

'That's right,' Claire replied. She looked into Terrill's eyes and saw, with understanding, a new look of deep happiness there. 'A real family. It's going to be so wonderful, isn't it?'

Terrill nodded. 'Which reminds me, Mrs Hawkes,' he said, a warm smile of contentment on his face as he moved Claire beneath him.

'Mmmm. Me too, Mr Hawkes,' Claire replied, as her arms closed around him.

Harlequin Superromance

**Here are the longer, more involving stories you
have been waiting for... Superromance.**

Modern, believable novels of love, full of the complex
joys and heartaches of real people.

Intriguing conflicts based on today's constantly
changing life-styles.

Four new titles every month.
Available wherever paperbacks are sold.

SUPER-1

# Harlequin Intrigue.

They went in through the terrace door. The house was dark, most of the servants were down at the circus, and only Nelbert's hired security guards were in sight. It was child's play for Blackheart to move past them, the work of two seconds to go through the solid lock on the terrace door. And then they were creeping through the darkened house, up the long curving stairs, Ferris fully as noiseless as the more experienced Blackheart.

They stopped on the second floor landing. "What if they have guns?" Ferris mouthed silently.

Blackheart shrugged. "Then duck."

"How reassuring," she responded. Footsteps directly above them signaled that the thieves were on the move, and so should they be.

For more romance, suspense and adventure, read Harlequin Intrigue. Two exciting titles each month, available wherever Harlequin Books are sold.

INTA-1

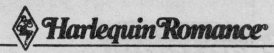
Harlequin Romance

Coming Next Month

2977 RANSOMED HEART Ann Charlton
Hal Stevens, hired by her wealthy father to protect Stacey, wastes no time in letting her know he considers her a spoiled brat and her life-style useless. But Stacey learns that even heiresses can't have everything they want....

2978 SONG OF LOVE Rachel Elliott
Claire Silver hadn't known Roddy Mackenzie very long—yet staying in his Scottish castle was just long enough to fall in love with him. Then suddenly Roddy is treating her as if he thinks she's using him. Has he had a change of heart?

2979 THE WILD SIDE Diana Hamilton
Hannah should have been on holiday in Morocco. Instead, she finds herself kidnapped to a snowbound cottage in Norfolk by a total stranger. And yet Waldo Ross seems to know all about Hannah.

2980 WITHOUT RAINBOWS Virginia Hart
Penny intends to persuade her father, Lon, to give up his dangerous obsession with treasure hunting. She *doesn't* intend to fall in love with Steffan Korda again—especially since he's financing Lon's next expedition in the Greek islands.

2981 ALIEN MOONLIGHT Kate Kingston
Petra welcomes the temporary job as nanny to three children in France as an escape from her ex-fiancé's attentions. She hasn't counted on Adam Herrald, the children's uncle. Sparks fly whenever they meet. But why does he dislike her?

2982 WHEN THE LOVING STOPPED Jessica Steele
It is entirely Whitney's fault that businessman Sloan Illingworth's engagement has ended disastrously. It seems only fair that she should make amends. Expecting her to take his fiancée's place in his life, however, seems going a bit too far!

Keepsake

 Harlequin Books

You're never too young to enjoy romance. Harlequin for you . . . and Keepsake, young-adult romances destined to win hearts, for your daughter.

Pick one up today and start your daughter on her journey into the wonderful world of romance.

Two new titles to choose from each month.